The Secret of the Seven Crows

Also by Wylly Folk St. John

Uncle Robert's Secret
The Mystery of the Other Girl
The Christmas Tree Mystery
The Mystery of the Gingerbread House
The Secrets of Pirate Inn
The Secrets of Hidden Creek

The Secret of the Seven Crows

WYLLY FOLK ST. JOHN

Illustrated by Judith Gwyn Brown

THE VIKING PRESS   NEW YORK

First Edition

Copyright © 1973 by Wylly Folk St. John
Illustrations copyright © 1973 by The Viking Press, Inc.
All rights reserved
First published in 1973 by The Viking Press, Inc.
625 Madison Avenue, New York, N.Y. 10022
Published simultaneously in Canada by
The Macmillan Company of Canada Limited
Library of Congress catalog card number: 73–5142

PRINTED IN U.S.A.

FIC   SBN 670–62992–8

1   2   3   4   5   77   76   75   74   73

This book, with love, is for the real Shelley and Pam, and for Becky, who discovered Crauleia for me

Contents

One crow means sorrow,
Two crows mean joy,
Three crows a wedding,
Four crows a boy.
Five crows mean silver,
Six crows mean gold,
Seven crows a secret
That's never been told.

OLD FOLK RHYME

The Scariest
Place They Ever Lived

Shelley asked her brother Jason, "Are you scared to go in?"

There was something mighty spooky about that huge old clapboard structure behind the sand dunes and the sea oats. It was as gray as the stormy twilight sky behind it and the rolling waves of the Gulf in front of it and the Spanish moss that hung on the bent and twisted live oak and cedar trees all around it.

She thought, if we really do come here tomorrow to stay, it'll be the scariest place we ever lived. And she knew they were going to live here, because the big U-Drive-It van with all their stuff in it was parked beside their car at the motel down the beach, on the edge of the little town of Gulf Springs. Daddy, with Jason and Otto and Bug to keep him company, had driven the van. Mama drove the car, with Pam and Shelley and Grandma and Pam's turtle Rover.

"Are you scared?" she asked again, because Jason

hadn't answered.

"No," he said at last. "But maybe you girls and Bug had better wait here till I go in first with Otto and see if there's anything to be scared of."

Jason was fourteen, but Shelley thought that just because he was two years ahead of her and their cousin Pam he didn't have any right to keep them out of scary places.

"Otto's very pregnant," she pointed out. "I don't believe she'd be as much help as we would if there's something dangerous in there. I'm coming too. So's Pam. So's Grandma." She hugged the gray striped cat tighter in her arms, and Grandma purred affirmatively. Pam just nodded, but it was an emphatic nod that made her reddish pigtails bounce.

"Me too," said Bug, who was nine and not about to be left by himself on the outside of any scary place.

Jason said soothingly to Otto, "Good dog!" in case Shelley might have hurt her feelings. Otto was a fine half police dog, and Jason felt sure she could bite all right even though she was about to have police dog–coon hound puppies any minute. He patted her head consolingly.

The four of them—six, counting Otto and Grandma (Pam had been persuaded to leave Rover in his bowl back at the motel)—were standing in front of a three-storied, abandoned, and weather-beaten building. Daddy had said, when he was first describing it to them, that it looked like a Victorian summer resort hotel, but it had actually been a convent retirement home for aged nuns before Hurricane Camille had flattened most of this part of the Gulf Coast a few summers ago. Houses and stores along the coast had been knocked down, trees twisted and uprooted, and though the larger towns had been partly rebuilt, the little settlement of Gulf Springs, not far from Biloxi, was still very much the way the wind and the waves had left it—desolate-looking, piled up with storm wreckage.

Shelley couldn't see why Daddy would want to have a boarding school here. True, this particular house seemed not to have been touched by the hurricane, but it didn't have much else to recommend it that she could see. At the back one enormous cedar tree, with most of its roots in the air while a few clung to the ground, leaned dangerously toward the house.

"Well, let's go in," Pam said. "You all couldn't wait till tomorrow to see it. So let's see it." Pam had come along with the Calhouns for the summer because she had never been to the beach, and she was Shelley's best friend besides being her first cousin, and Daddy said there was certainly plenty of room at St. Mary's Convent even if there wasn't much of anything else.

"Come on." Shelley was impatient too. "It'll be dark pretty soon. We wouldn't want to be here in the dark. And there's going to be a storm. See that black cloud?"

They started up a drive that was overgrown with wiregrass and cockspurs. Their feet sank into white sand that felt grainy when it got inside their sneakers.

Otto whined, and began gnawing at her front paw, until Jason found a cockspur between the pads and took it out.

The old convent stood on a spot higher than the surrounding beachfront, so that it seemed to tower over everything, even the moss-hung live oaks and cedars and palmettos of the tangled woods behind it. At one side in back of the main building stood a smaller house, maybe a one-room servant's cottage, Shelley thought, and another outbuilding that could have been a carriage house or, more recently, a garage. Except that nuns didn't have servants or carriages or cars. But maybe whoever lived in the house before the nuns came, did.

The screen wire around the long porch that was on three sides of the main building was loose and rusty. The porch's screen door dangled on its hinges, and a sudden wind slammed it back and forth. That was the only thing in the whole deserted landscape that moved, except some weird black birds that flew above the trees in back, and a forked tongue of lightning that flashed out of the dark clouds.

"It's all open," Bug said wonderingly as they walked across the porch. Their steps sounded loud on the creaky boards. "They didn't even shut the front door."

"Well, the nuns left in a hurry, because of the hurricane, Daddy said," Shelley reminded him. "And when I asked him why they never came back, he said he guessed they were just too old and discouraged. Maybe they didn't like hurricane country."

They straggled down the porch to the door and peered warily inside, then cautiously advanced. The rooms were large, shadowy, and empty. Opening out from the center entrance hall stretched a long passageway in either direction, with several rooms on both sides. On the whole, the place was surprisingly clean. The nuns didn't have so much to take with them when the hurricane came, Shelley mused. Nuns never had anything but the barest necessities. No hair rollers to gather up, no stuffed animals on their beds, no trinkets, hardly any clothes. Or furniture. So they wouldn't have left much trash. The voices and footsteps of the four echoed in the emptiness.

"It seems like a home for old nuns, all right," Jason said, wrinkling his nose. It smelled musty and like old sea water at the same time.

"Oh, I don't know," Shelley said. "I can imagine it would have been somebody's home once, before it was a convent. See, this room has a fireplace, and so did the last one. It has shelves like a library. I think these downstairs rooms were once even bigger; then they were divided. Probably one was a ballroom, before the nuns took it over."

At the end of the passage there was an abrupt turn into a smaller passage. Jason, who was ahead, gave a gasp, and Pam behind him a small startled scream. There in the dusk somebody was standing.

It took a minute to see that he was standing too still to be alive. He was a statue—a bearded figure with a child in his arms. His long robe was brown over white;

he held two golden lilies and a gold cross, besides the baby Jesus, who had a halo over His head.

Shelley, behind the others, hurriedly clutched Grandma in her left arm, and made the sign of the cross. The Calhouns weren't Catholic but they had friends who were, and Shelley had always secretly envied Mary Eileen that quick gesture of silent prayer which would surely ward off evil. She had adopted it for her own—but only when nobody could see her. They would think it was funny. Nobody would understand—except God. She had every confidence that He would, even if Pam wouldn't.

"It must be Joseph," Jason said.

"Yes," Shelley agreed. "If the convent was named St. Mary's, then Joseph would be around. I think they called him St. Joseph, though." She saw Bug reach out and gently touch the Baby's foot, and she wanted to hug him for doing it.

"Look!" Pam said, her blue eyes widening.

Through an open door they could see a small room, the only one so far that wasn't bare. They stood at the door and took it all in. There was one small, beautiful stained-glass window—a panel of white lilies surrounded by ruby and sapphire and emerald panes, leaded between. The white walls behind an altar were painted with blue sky, small white clouds, and several cherubs. The dark wainscoting around the other walls had a molding to edge it, intricately carved. There were eight carved pews of the dark wood, four on each side of the narrow aisle. Behind the altar hung a large crucifix, and at the right of it stood a life-sized statue of the Madonna and Child. Even though twilight was turning toward night, Shelley could see that her robe was the proper blue.

"It looks like a church," Bug guessed.

"Silly, it's their chapel," Shelley said.

"What's the thing that looks like a bird bath?" Bug pointed to the other corner beside the altar.

"It's called a font. They keep holy water in it. But of course it's all dried up now."

"How do you know?"

"I went to the cathedral with Mary Eileen some-times, remember?"

"And what are the footstools for?" Bug was always curious.

Shelley answered, "They're for the nuns to kneel on when they pray. But—it's strange. Somebody took all the stuff from the other rooms away. But seems like they left everything that was in the chapel just like it belonged."

"Maybe," Jason surmised, "the nuns hurried away when the hurricane was coming, and didn't have time to take anything. Then something happened to them —they could have died in the storm; lots of people did, Dad said—and later somebody else looted the place. But whoever was stealing stuff was afraid to touch the chapel, with St. Joseph standing guard over it."

"Yes!" Shelley's imagination leaped ahead of him. "And I bet when the nuns were leaving, the Mother Superior took a minute to stop in the chapel and ask the Blessed Virgin and St. Joseph not to let the hurricane destroy the convent. That's probably why it wasn't smashed like everything else around here."

"Are we going to have a church right in our house when we live here?" Bug asked. "That'll be neat, won't it?"

"Great," Shelley agreed.

"Will we have a tame preacher too?"

"You mean our own chaplain? I don't much think so—though it's not a bad idea, is it, for a school to have a resident chaplain?"

"Let's see what's upstairs," Jason said. "It's about to get dark, and Mama and Dad will be looking for us."

"Do you think the stairs are safe?" Pam asked when they found a wide flight of steps at the other side of the passage.

"They seem solid enough," Jason said, stamping on the lowest step. The echo of his thump came back eerily, along with a growl of thunder. "Dad said houses were built of stronger materials in the old days."

"It's kind of scary, isn't it?" Pam said. "I wish there were some lights we could turn on."

"We'll hurry. We can't see much tonight. We'll explore better tomorrow. But we do want to just take a look. Yeah, it's spooky all right."

They hurried through the second floor rooms—small empty rooms, that could have been individual bedrooms made by dividing larger rooms—and the bathrooms at each end, with old-fashioned tubs still in place, standing on feet that looked like lions' paws.

There was another flight of stairs at the opposite end
of the long hall, and both ends had another flight lead-
ing to the third floor. The vacant rooms up there were
even smaller.

"They must have had lots of nuns here," Pam
guessed.

"Probably not all the rooms were used," Shelley
suggested. "The chapel couldn't have held nearly as
many as the bedrooms could."

"Well," Pam said as they were going back down the
stairs, "I don't know why Uncle Jonathan would want
this old dump."

Shelley told her, "Maybe you don't realize how
much he's always wanted a school of his own, Pam,
but we've always known it. Even when he was in
college he dreamed about having one, and took the
right courses and got his degree so he could teach.
And when he was on the paper he thought about it,
but he didn't make enough money to buy a school.
Then when he was at Lockheed and making more
money, he still thought about it and started saving for
it. And when he got laid off at Lockheed, because they
had to cut down expenses and didn't need so many
public-relations men, he got his money out of the
retirement fund and decided to take a chance and have
a school at last. Private schools are a big thing right
now, I heard him tell Mama—but of course they've got
to be integrated."

"What's integrated?" Bug asked.

"Oh, Bug, you know that. It means we'll have black

and white children both. Chinese, too, and Indians, if
they want to come."

"Tough!" Bug said happily. "I never knew any
Indians personally. Or Chinese either."

They were back on the ground floor now.

"Hey," Jason said, "there.are some more steps. Going down. Looks dark down there. No windows on
these stairs."

"Let's take a quick look down there anyhow,"
Shelley said.

They emerged into a big room with brick walls,
a door at ground level, and windows that opened into
the back yard. A little light still came in. Dusty curtains still hung here—brown-checked curtains. There
were two ranges at the far end, an electric one (though
an early model) and an old-fashioned wood-burning
iron cookstove, and in the corner a large niche with
shelves. Other open shelves were against the walls.
Two long, plain wooden tables were placed down the
center of the room. A double sink stood under one
window. On a nail behind the door hung something
that Shelley identified as a blue gingham apron, a
large one. She had never before thought of nuns as
wearing aprons when they cooked—but of course, she
told herself, they would.

The floor was of brick, too. Footsteps sounded different down here, as the four, along with Grandma and
Otto, went to the end of the room to investigate the
cooking arrangements.

"I guess the stoves and tables—and those tubs and

all upstairs—were too big to steal when the vandals were plundering," Jason said. On one table was what seemed to be the remains of a meal—no food, but dishes and cutlery that hadn't been washed, opened cans and fruit jars, and dirty glasses. "Somebody ate here, but it wasn't the nuns," he guessed.

"Do you think you could cook on that thing?" Shelley asked him, staring at the huge iron stove. Jason's hobby was cooking, but he cooked mostly things with French names and fancy recipes. Mama called it his French-chef-galloping-gourmet phase.

"I doubt it. Not my chocolate soufflé, anyhow."

"It was probably tramps who ate here, or the people that stole all the stuff," Shelley said. "And rats got the rest of the food. Look—there was probably more food left in the pantry, on those shelves, when the hurricane came. Probably lots of jars of stuff the nuns pre-served, but somebody took it. All they left was that can of nutmeg there and that jar of something that got broken." She had a sad feeling, thinking of how hard the nuns (in blue gingham aprons!) had worked pre-serving and canning that food. And then to have to leave it because of the hurricane! And somebody else coming along and stealing it—

"Look," Pam said, "there's a calendar on the wall."

"And look at the month—August, 1969. I'm almost sure that was when the hurricane struck." Shelley stared at it, shuddering, feeling how it was in August, 1969, when the aged nuns under this roof heard the great roar of the wind that meant swift disaster and the end of their peaceful life here.

"It's got to be—unless somebody's lived here since."

"Nobody's lived here since, Daddy said."

Jason said suddenly, "What's that? I hear something—listen!"

Shelley's heart thumped, and for a minute that was all she could hear. Bug's hand clutched her arm, and she heard him stop breathing. Then in the gloom she saw Pam's pale face, and Jason's lifted to listen. Otto growled, low in her throat.

Shelley heard it now. Footsteps. Overhead.

Somebody else was in the darkening house with them. Or—ghosts? It was a spooky house, and the footsteps weren't very heavy footsteps. They sounded kind of—unreal.

The back door hung ajar.

"Let's run for it," Pam breathed.

Otto barked, her rapid loud bark that was her fierce warning to strangers not to approach her family. The sudden bark startled Grandma, and she leaped right out of Shelley's arms. Before Shelley could grab her, she had dashed back up those dark stairs.

Jason and the others had already started for the back door. Shelley whispered as loud as she could whisper —not thinking why she whispered—"Jason! We can't run for it. Grandma's gone back upstairs. I've got to go after her."

Jason stopped. He knew they ought to get out while they could. But they couldn't desert Grandma. Shelley was already hurrying toward the stairs.

"All right," he said. "No use whispering with Otto making all that noise. Come on. Everybody stay together. Maybe it's not anybody but—maybe Daddy coming to look for us—"

But they all knew it wasn't Daddy. The footsteps weren't heavy enough to be Daddy's.

They crept up the stairs, holding onto each other in the dark, stumbling over Otto, who kept on barking. Shelley thought, there'll be a little more light at the top.

Then, when Otto stopped barking for a minute, there came a strange, hoarse loud cry in the dead air—like a scream, only not quite like a scream either. Like nothing they had ever heard before.

"What's that?" Pam gasped.

How Can Seven
Crows Have a Secret?

"I don't know what it is," Bug said in a small voice. "But I don't like it. I want to go home."

Shelley said, "No help, Bug. This *is* home." Suddenly realizing it, she sounded desolate even to herself.

Jason had stopped unexpectedly at the top of the stairs, and Pam, behind him, had bumped into him. Looking ahead over his shoulder, she gasped again. "What's that?"

"Do you see something?" Shelley whispered. "A ghost?" Then she could see it too, and it did look like an apparition. But it was silhouetted dark against the faint light of one of those tall first-floor windows, and of course ghosts weren't solid enough to have silhouettes. It looked like somebody standing there, a thin, quite still somebody, with—could it be?—a large, quite still bird on one shoulder. Then the bird let out another hoarse caw and she recognized it. A crow! That was the cry they had heard.

"It's a girl," Jason said, and Shelley heard him let out a deep breath of relief. "I think." He went up the last step, and they came after him. The girl still stood there without saying anything. Weird.

"Are you a girl?" Pam said at last.

"What do you think?"

When she spoke, it was in quite an ordinary girl's voice. As tall as Jason, she had on jeans and a man's shirt that hung down over them, loose on her skinny frame. Shelley could see now that her hair was in sandy wisps around her narrow face, and her eyes were the strangest light green she had ever seen. Shelley's own eyes were what Mama called hazel, and had some green in their brown, like a forest pool. She had always liked to fancy herself as having green eyes. But hers were nothing like the strange pale color of this girl's, almost like a cat's in the dim light.

As she thought that, she remembered Grandma, the reason they had come back up here instead of running away. "Grandma! Where are you? Here, Grandma! Here, kitty, kitty, kitty—"

"There she is!" Bug said. "And look—Grandma's got a mouse in her mouth!" He pointed toward the hall door. Sure enough, there she was.

The strange girl laughed and put a hand on her crow. Shelley guessed the crow had been startled by Grandma when the cat first ran up the stairs. Of course. That was why it had squawked. Now the girl and the bird didn't seem so unfriendly, only—well, still strange.

"I won't let her hurt your crow," Shelley said reassuringly.

"Then I won't let him hurt your cat. I mean your grandma." The girl laughed again, and Shelley laughed too. She could see it would seem like a right funny name for a cat. They still hadn't told their faraway grandmother that Bug had named the kitten after her because he loved both of them so much.

"What's his name?" Shelley reached for the crow; he fluttered his wings and she took back her hand.

"Dracula," the girl said ominously. "He *may* be part vampire."

Shelley felt Bug's hand tighten on her arm again. "Not really," she told Bug. "She doesn't mean really."

"That's what you think." The cool green eyes looked amused; the sharp chin tilted provokingly.

"Dracula, Blackula," Shelley said. "Bet you had a hard time taming him."

"No trouble at all. Crows belong to us. We belong to them."

It was a funny thing to say. Shelley felt goose bumps on her arms. "What's your name?" she asked. "I'm Shelley Calhoun. This is my brother Jason, and this is my brother Bug. And our cousin, Pam Jones. And our dog Otto. You already met Grandma."

"I'm Gale. Gale Franklin. I was born in a hurricane; that's why I was named Gale—What are you doing here at Crauleia?" she asked abruptly.

"I thought this was St. Mary's," Jason said.

"It was Crauleia before it was St. Mary's. It'll always be Crauleia. What are you all doing here?"

"We're going to live here."

"Oh." Gale looked them over again: three dark-haired with dark eyes, one red-haired with blue eyes. "My father didn't say— I mean, I knew somebody was coming, but—"

"Is it your father who owns this place?" Shelley asked.

"We own it," Gale said. "Sort of. My great-great-great-grandmother built it, way back before 1900. She was Mrs. Howard Townsend Crawley, and all I know about her is that she was rich and she was crazy. Crazy about crows. She named it Crauleia; it means Crows' Wood. There are still a lot of crows in the woods be-tween this and our house. That's where the name Crawley came from, too—from crows—way back in County Sussex, in England. There was a Crawley there in 1203. My mother was a Crawley before she married. We had to have a smaller place to live than Crauleia, of course."

"Why won't your father sell this place to us?" Shelley asked. "He doesn't seem to care anything about it—look at it!—but Daddy said he won't sell it. He told Daddy we can live in it all summer—free—and fix it up any way we want, and if we still want to stay when summer is over, we can rent it cheap. Nobody else would have it. But your father wouldn't sell it, and Daddy kind of wonders about sinking all his money in a place that doesn't actually belong to him."

"Why does your father want it?" Gale asked suspiciously.

The light was almost gone from the windows now, and Bug had Grandma safe in his arms—without the mouse—but Shelley took time to tell her. "It's a romantic story," she said. "He heard about this house from a soldier in Vietnam a few years ago when Daddy was on the paper and went over there as a correspondent. He had made friends with the soldier— Why, yes! His name was Crawley!"

"That would be my Uncle Sol," Gale said. "He was killed in Vietnam."

"While they were just sitting around the base waiting for the shooting to begin, Daddy and your uncle talked a lot. Daddy told him about how he'd always wanted to own a school, and your uncle said he knew a perfect place for a school. He told Daddy everything about it, about the nuns and all. He did say it wasn't for sale, though. Daddy forgot all about it till he got laid off from Lockheed and had a little money saved up, and the pension plan money, and thought he was ready to start his school at last. Then he remembered St. Mary's and came to see if by any chance it was vacant and for sale. He thought it would do fine, and came back for us. He wants it very much. So why won't your father sell it?"

"I wish we could," Gale said. "Then maybe we'd have enough money to fix up our house. The hurricane took off the whole back part of it, and we have to live in the few rooms left. But we can't sell it, you see, until we find whatever it is Great-great-great-grandmother hid here. I told you she was crazy. Nothing she did would surprise me. In her will she left this house 'and all that's in it and around it' to whichever of her descendants is bright enough to figure out what 'the secret of the seven crows' is. Until then, it's all held in trust, and she left enough money in trust, too, to pay the taxes, but not any for repairs.

"Nobody has even come close to figuring out the secret yet. But before my mother died she begged my father to go on looking for whatever is hidden here, for me. She made him promise. She thought it was something very valuable, like a hidden treasure. He's about given up looking for it, though. But I haven't."

Shelley was almost breathless with excitement. "Can we help you look?" she begged. "The secret of the seven crows! I don't think your uncle told Daddy that part. A secret treasure! That'll really be something to spend the summer doing. We have to help Daddy paint and repair and fix up the school, of course. But there'll be lots of spare time. Can we help hunt for it?"

Gale shrugged. "Be my guest," she said. "But it's only fair to warn you, I don't think my great-great-great-grandmother would like for anybody to find it but me. She wants in the worst way for somebody of her own blood to find where she hid it. She wants to help me find it before a stranger gets it. I'm the last one left, you see, after Mama and Uncle Sol died. So I'd have to be the one, if anybody in the family is to find it. At least, that's my theory about why she's still hanging around here."

"You mean—her ghost is still here?" Shelley

breathed, her spine feeling chilly all the way from her tailbone to her hair.

"We don't believe in ghosts," Jason said disapprovingly to Shelley.

Gale shook her head at him. "Then I doubt if you could ever see her," she said. "People who don't believe in ghosts never see them."

Shelley said, "I think I believe in them, Gale! At least, I get goose bumps when I think about them. Do you really think your great-great-great-grandma's ghost is here? Now?"

"I don't know whether to think that or not," Gale said. "People say so. I never saw her myself, though I come here often, hoping to. Maybe it's just a legend. You know how people talk when a house is unoccupied. But ever since she died, as an old lady, years and years ago, nobody would ever stay here long, until the nuns came. They aren't afraid of ghosts, it seems."

Shelley nodded. "They just cross themselves and are safe from being afraid."

"I don't think I'd be afraid of Mrs. Howard Townsend Crawley," Gale said thoughtfully, "dead or alive. Especially if I had Dracula with me. She liked crows too. She had a pet crow named Beelzebub, they said. I wish I could see her ghost. And Beelzebub's. I'd just ask her to help me with the clues. Of course, she might have forgotten, herself, where she hid whatever it is. It was a long time ago."

"Clues?" Jason said. He had been listening with interest, but not talking much. He wanted Shelley to get through yakking with this weird girl and come on back to the motel. But now the mention of clues caught him. He liked to read detective stories almost as much as he liked to cook. "What clues?"

"Will you let me be the one to find it at the last—if we do it together?" Gale bargained, looking from one to the other of them. "I mean, even if you figure it out, will you let me be the one to look at it first—whatever the treasure is? If I tell you the clues?"

"Of course," Jason said kindly. "All we'd want would be just the fun of looking for it. The treasure's yours."

"Well, I want to find it for more reason than that," Shelley said. "Of course whatever it is would be yours, Gale, and you could see it first. But I want to find it so your father will be able to sell the place to Daddy, because Daddy wants it so much. It would just fix everything up for everybody, if we could only find it!" she said longingly. "You'd have the money to rebuild your house, from the sale of this place as well as whatever treasure Mrs. Crawley hid for you. And Daddy'd have his school."

"And maybe I could have something to eat," Bug said plaintively. "I'm starving, Shelley."

"Me, too," Pam said.

"Wait," Shelley begged. "Let her tell us about the clues. Then we could be thinking about them all night, and be ready to start searching in the morning."

But a great clap of thunder startled them all, before Gale could start telling. "There's going to be a big storm," she exclaimed. "And Taz and Raymond's father went out on his shrimp boat for one of those several-night trips, and he'll be caught in it. Roscoe too. Those kids will be scared to death. I don't know why he bothers to go out; he hardly ever brings back any shrimp. But Roscoe gets enough fish for them to eat. Sometimes they give us some. But not the shrimp when he catches any—they're too scarce and expensive this year."

"Who're Taz and Raymond? And Roscoe?" Pam asked.

But Jason said impatiently, "The clues, the clues, kid!"

Gale didn't mind tantalizing him. "Taz and Raymond Willis are friends of mine, and so are Roscoe's kids, Michael and Patricia. Roscoe is Cap'n Boney's deck man. Roscoe Lummus. They live in trailers over at the trailer park. They always think the *St. Boniface* won't make it back when there's a storm."

"The *St. Boniface?*" It didn't sound like a boat's name.

"It's the only one of the shrimp fleet that isn't named for a woman. Cap'n Boney named it for himself. He's got a crazy name, Boniface. He was named for a Catholic saint, Taz says. I ought to go see if he and Raymond are scared."

"Well, their mother will take care of them, won't she?"

"Taz and Raymond don't have any mother; Cap'n Boney divorced her. He got custody. They stay by themselves at the trailer. But when he's going to be away he pays Michael and Patricia's mother to give them their meals and kind of look after them. He doesn't just leave them, like some guys would do."

"Are they real special friends of yours?" Shelley asked. "Like hunting-for-the-secret kind of friends?"

"No, not like that," Gale reassured her. "They don't know anything about that. They aren't really old enough. They're more his size," she said, nodding at Bug. "I guess Taz is about ten or eleven; he's the oldest."

Jason had had enough of Cap'n Boney Willis and his gross old shrimp boat. "Are you going to tell us about those clues, or not?" he demanded.

Gale could be contrary when she was pushed.

"I've got to go now," she said. "Dracula doesn't like to be out in storms. If it doesn't turn out to be one of those storms that lasts all day tomorrow too, I'll meet you in the Crows' Wood about ten. Maybe I'll tell you then."

"Maybe we won't be there, either," Jason retorted.

"I will!" Shelley said earnestly. "I'll be there, Gale! So will Pam. We've just got to find out about the secret of the seven crows."

"O.K.," Gale said. She was gone so quickly that it almost seemed as if she had disappeared like a—ghost.

Shelley had been so engrossed in what Gale was saying that she hadn't realized how dark it was getting. Now they could hardly find their way across the porch, fumbling along the broken railing, looking back fearfully, almost running—because they could imagine the ghost of an old woman and the ghosts of seven crows lurking in the shadows. The beach and the water glimmered vaguely out there when the lightning crackled. It was low tide, and the wet stretch of sand shone like silver at every flash.

"Here, let me take Grandma," Shelley said to Bug as they reached Crauleia's driveway. "We've got to run for it."

"We shouldn't be out on the open beach in a thunderstorm," Jason panted. "We could get struck by lightning—it's dangerous. But I don't see how we can get back to the motel if we don't take the beach—the road's just as open, and we can run faster on the wet part where the sand's not soft." He turned back and picked up Otto, because she couldn't waddle fast enough.

"Come on!"

Now they were running, their feet pounding on the wet sand, the loose dark hair of three of them blowing back in the wind, and Pam's red pigtails bouncing. Bug stumbled and fell, and Pam swooped back and picked him up and held his hand as they ran on. The rain was in their faces now, wild and swirling. If there were any ghosts, they had been left behind for the time being. Shelley felt suddenly exultant. She thought, I can't stand it, it's so exciting!

She panted, "Jason! How can seven crows have a secret?"

He looked back at her over his shoulder as he ran, across the bulky dog he was carrying. He looked wild and excited too, now, though he had kept his cool when they were with Gale.

"I don't know," he gasped. "But, Shell, we'll find out!"

The Clues in the Rhyme

The storm was over by morning; the sun shone and Crauleia looked different when the Calhouns arrived very early to move in. It didn't look so weird now, only abandoned.

Shelley saw how enthusiastic Daddy was about the old place, but Mama didn't think much of the nuns' big old kitchen. "First thing, get the electricity and water turned on," she urged. "Then we can see if the electric stove works. Jason and I can't cook on that monster of a wood stove."

"I'll go into the town and do that," Daddy agreed, "and try to find a couple of men to help us move the furniture in. You all can be cleaning up the few rooms we're going to live in while we work on the school part. Jason, you want to come with me?"

"Sure, Dad."

They took the car. Shelley watched them with the usual small ache in her heart. She wasn't jealous, she was sure. But Daddy almost always took Jason. She didn't blame him; she guessed she would have loved Jason best, herself. But it would have been so great if Daddy happened to love Shelley as much as he loved Jason. Of course, he often hugged Shelley and kissed her and she never doubted that he really loved her too. But not quite the same way. Well, she told herself, Jason was the oldest. And of course, she figured, Mama loved Bug best because he was the baby. Shelley was the middle child, and it wasn't easy.

But if she could be the one to find out the secret of the seven crows and get Crauleia free for Daddy to buy, that would surely please him, she thought. Maybe he'd say, "Look, Shelley got the place for us!" Maybe he'd name it The Shelley School. Maybe he'd put his hand carelessly over hers all the time, the way he did once. She shut her eyes and wished in the intense way she wished for very important things. *The secret of the seven crows.* I've got to find it.

"What are you standing there like that for?" Pam asked. "You look so funny. What are you thinking about?"

"Nothing," Shelley said. She grabbed a laundry basket full of stuff to carry in the house. "Come on, let's pick out a room to be ours, and start cleaning it. You sweep and dust and I'll mop. We have to get away at ten, you know, to meet Gale in the woods."

"That weird kid!" Pam said. "You didn't believe all that stuff she was saying, did you?"

"Of course I believe her. If you don't believe in weird things, it isn't any fun."

"Well, I'll go, but I don't have to believe everything she says." Pam looked around for a bucket and mop. "Hey, we forgot. We can't do much till the water gets turned on."

"Well, we can sweep and then carry stuff in."

Mama said they might as well pile it all in the wide hall until they got the rooms clean, which would take a while even after they got water. They worked hard till they saw the car coming back.

The service men would be out soon, Daddy reported, to turn on the utilities. But it wasn't so easy to find men to help them move the heavy furniture in. "Nobody around here seems to want the job," Daddy said, "even though they're loafing around the docks not doing anything. Talk about the unemployed!"

Shelley said, "It's because of the ghost. Probably they're scared to work here, Daddy."

"What ghost?"

"Didn't you tell him about Mrs. Crawley, Jason? She's the old lady who built Crauleia—that was the name of this house before it was St. Mary's. She's still here. We met a girl last night—her father is Mr. Franklin, the one you saw about living here. Her uncle was your soldier friend in Vietnam. She told us about her great-great-great-grandmother who built the house. And we're supposed to meet her—Gale Franklin, not Mrs. Crawley's ghost—at ten this morning in the woods and she'll tell us some more."

Jason said, "It didn't seem real, this morning. We were talking about so many real things, I guess I never thought about mentioning it."

"Well, that hidden whatever-it-is sounds real to me," Shelley said wistfully. "And it sure would help out if we could find it. Daddy, Mr. Franklin didn't tell you the real reason he won't sell the place, I guess. It's because old Mrs. Crawley hid something that's very valuable around here somewhere. After we find it, he'll be glad to sell. At least, Gale thinks so. You'd be glad if we found it, wouldn't you?"

"I certainly would," Daddy said. "This is the only place I've seen that would do for a school that I might be able to afford to buy. And you might as well go and meet your friend because we can't accomplish much about that cleaning-up job till we get some water. I'm going back to town again to try to find somebody who isn't afraid of work—or ghosts!"

"Put mine and Pam's stuff in the room at the top of the stairs, please," Shelley said. "Jason, I wish you and Bug would have the one next to us. And Mama, I wish you and Daddy would sleep right across the hall from us, so we could call you if we got scared."

"That's a good idea," Mama said. "And let's make our living room the one downstairs at the same end of the hall—and the same end where the steps go down to the kitchen. Then all our living quarters

will be together, though on different levels, and
apart from the school, in a way."

"Good—that'll put the chapel at our end too,"
Shelley said. "I like that chapel."

"It's going to be easy to fix up the school office and
library and classrooms and dormitory rooms in the
rest of the house," Daddy said. "Even if we have to
do most of the work ourselves."

"We're going to help," Shelley said. "But won't we
need experts for things like plumbing and wiring?"

"I might try the carpentering myself. But surely I
can find men who aren't afraid of ghosts to do the
plumbing and wiring," Daddy said. "But right now I'm
just looking for some husky men who can lift that big
old sofa of ours."

He went off, not taking Jason this time.

Jason said to Mama, "Would you be afraid, if we
all went to meet that weird kid in the woods and left
you by yourself? She was going to tell us the clues
her great-great-great-grandmother left, about how to
find whatever she hid in this house. Otto can stay to
protect you. And we don't need Grandma," he told
Shelley.

"I'm not afraid," Mama assured him.

"I buttered Grandma's paws," Shelley said, "and
she's too busy licking the butter off to go anywhere.
That's the way to make a cat know she's at home,
when it's a new place, isn't it, Mama?"

"Right," Mama said. "Grandma and I will be fine.
And Otto."

"Otto knows even if you don't butter her paws," Jason said. "She's got sense. She knows wherever we live is home."

"Come on, you all," Shelley said. "It's nearly ten."

The Crows' Wood was eerie. So many of the big old live oaks had been killed or uprooted or twisted by the hurricane that they were dead agonized gray skeletons of trees, draped with graybeard moss that made them look as if monster spiders had been hanging webs on them. The moss too was dead. Jason, who read everything, said Spanish moss was a parasite that had to live on living trees. A few of the tree trunks had sprouted new limbs, and there was an especially tall and wide one that seemed to have been untouched by the damaging wind. It spread green sheltering arms above a big circle of shade. Pines, too, had been tossed around and lay at odd angles across other dead trees, their roots turned upward, but there were enough scrub pines and oaks left to make shady a little path that led between the fallen giants. Alongside it, green fans of palmettos were growing in clumps, and sweet myrtle—and always cockspurs and wiregrass.

And everywhere there were crows, great flocks of them. They flew off at the children's approach, but stayed, cawing, somewhere nearby.

Gale came meandering along another path that led from the opposite direction. Dracula was on her shoulder and seemed to be muttering in her ear.

"Hey, can Dracula talk?" Bug asked, even before the others could say hi.

"Hi," Gale said. "Sure he can talk. When he wants to."

"Make him say something."

Gale opened her greenish eyes wide, and shook her head at Bug. "Uh-uh. You don't make a crow like Dracula do anything. He does what he wants to, see? He's my familiar." She sat down on a fallen log. "This big tree is the Crows' Roost," she said. "They fly back here at night from miles around, to sleep."

"I thought only witches have familiars," Jason said.

"So?" Gale tilted her sharp chin at him.

But Shelley knew Gale was just putting Jason on. She was no witch. You had a feeling about some people—you knew they were going to be friends. Shelley had that feeling about Gale. She sat down on the log beside her. Pam sat too, on the sand. Jason leaned against a tree. Bug squatted in front of Gale, giving Dracula bits of cookie, trying to coax him into a conversation. "Say something!" he urged. "Nice Dracula—say something!"

Dracula fixed bright black eyes on Bug and suddenly opened his beak. In a hoarse voice he said, "Birds can't talk!" The sudden response startled Bug. He lost his balance and fell back off his heels, onto the sandy ground. Then he picked himself up, laughing at the bird. "They can too!" he said.

"Crows are very intelligent birds," Gale told Bug. "They stick together, too. If one gets shot in the air, the others fly around him and try with their wings and beaks to hold him up and keep him from a hard fall. And they post a sentinel to look out and warn the flock when hunters are coming. If the sentinel fails to do his job, they hold a court to try him. They sit around him in a circle, and if he's found guilty they all peck him, one at a time, and run him out of the flock. Once Mr. Dilmous Wilson saw a crow commit suicide after he had been cast out by the flock. He flew straight at a gun even while the hunter was firing at him."

"Who's Mr. Dilmous Wilson?" Shelley asked.

"A friend of mine. He used to be postmaster of Gulf Springs, but he retired and stays home now, except when he's out on the beach feeding the gulls. He whistles and they come to him like pigeons— thousands of them. Didn't you notice the gull tracks on the beach?"

"I did wonder what they were," Shelley said.

"Mr. Dilmous is a valuable man to have for a friend," Gale assured her. "He can tell you anything you need to know. He has loads of books, and he knows all kinds of great stuff about everything. Especially Shakespeare. He's a Shakespeare freak." Gale put up her forefinger to Dracula and he hopped onto it. She held him out to Bug, and Dracula stepped from her finger onto Bug's. Bug could hardly believe it; he caught his breath with joy.

"Hi, Dracula," he said softly. Shelley knew again that she liked Gale.

Pam said, "Would he come to me?"

"Try." Gale shrugged. But Dracula flew off, circled around, and landed again on Bug's finger. "Well, maybe after he gets to know you better," Gale told Pam.

Jason said—too bluntly, Shelley thought—"What about the clues? When are we going to start looking for—whatever we're looking for? That treasure of yours?"

"Oh, yes," Gale said, as if she'd just remembered. "I didn't tell you the clues last night, did I?"

"No, you didn't," Jason said, scowling, and Shelley was afraid he'd get tired of Gale's kidding him and decide not to help them after all.

"Come on, tell us, Gale," she said placatingly. "Did your great-great-great-grandmother really leave some clues to where you might find the secret of the seven crows? I don't see how you can live with something like that—it's so exciting! I'd be hunting every minute for the secret, if—"

"I've been hunting it all my life," Gale said. "Not exactly every minute, of course, and I couldn't do much when the nuns were here in Crauleia. But ever since the house has been empty, I've been looking. And in the priest's house, too. And I can't find a thing."

"The priest's house?"

"That little shack out in the back yard. That's where Father Bryan lived when the nuns were here."

"I thought maybe it was a servants' house."

"It was, when she built it. Then later she had a

boarder who lived—and died—there, my mother said. He was a strange old man—nobody knew much about him. There was some kind of mystery to it. Maybe he's a ghost now, too."

"Well, tell us the clues," Jason said impatiently. "And then we'll decide whether to help you find the stuff or not."

"We've already decided!" Pam and Shelley said together. "Of course we're going to."

Bug said, "Me too," but he added, "Maybe I could train me a crow like Dracula—" and Shelley could tell he didn't really have his mind on the subject of Gale's quest.

"O.K.," Gale said. "Here it is. It's a rhyme handed down in my family—they say my great-great-great-grandmother left this yellowed old piece of paper with her will that said 'the house and all that's in it and around it' should go to whichever descendant of hers could figure out the secret of the seven crows. But the paper is so old it's going to pieces, so my mother memorized it and so did I." She shut her eyes, concentrating, and chanted solemnly:

> One crow means sorrow,
> Two crows mean joy,
> Three crows a wedding,
> Four crows a boy.
> Five crows mean silver,
> Six crows mean gold,
> Seven crows a secret
> That's never been told.

Jason said, "The first part doesn't sound like clues to any treasure. Only the last part."

"I think the first part's just sort of family superstitions," Gale said. "My mother said she was told by her father that the night his great-grandmother was about to die, there was one crow that sat on a limb of that old cedar tree beside Crauleia all night until she died. It was a sign of death approaching. They said one crow has always showed up—'for sorrow'—every time somebody in the family was going to die. I saw it myself before my mother died. One crow—sitting on a tree limb outside her window." Her voice fell to a low, appropriate pitch. "One crow by itself is a sign of sorrow, all right."

"Or a coincidence," Jason said skeptically.

"Maybe when old Mrs. Crawley died, it was her pet crow Beelzebub waiting around for her," Pam surmised.

"No," Gale said. "Beelzebub had died first. That was one way they knew she was going to die, you see. When a person's familiar dies, he's not long for this world. I take great care of Dracula," she told them solemnly. "I'm not ready to die yet."

"Are you kidding me?" Shelley demanded. "You mean—?"

Gale nodded, without a smile. "The crow is our clan token," she said. "I guess you don't know about clan tokens? Mr. Dilmous Wilson does. Crows that are familiars are different from the other crows. You can tell if they hold up one claw, for instance, when a hunter is about to shoot them. If he's an enemy he shoots anyway and the person dies if the crow dies. But if he's a friend he lets it live. Sometimes a whole species is spared because the clan isn't sure which ones are their familiars. That's why there are so many crows around Crauleia, I figure. My mother and Uncle Sol and all didn't know which one was theirs; so they protected all of them. But I know." She reached out and stroked Dracula's head. "And Mrs. Howard Townsend Crawley did."

"Your father doesn't have one?"

"No, because he's not a Crawley, see?"

"Did you see one crow," Shelley asked, "when your uncle was killed in Vietnam?"

"Of course. That was how we knew, even before the officer came to tell us."

"It's pretty easy to see a crow around here," Jason said. "In fact it'd be pretty hard not to."

"Not one by himself," Gale retorted, "unless he's a sentinel or has been exiled by the flock. They stay in flocks. And of course the sentinels aren't around the house. That's where you have to see them if it's a sign somebody's going to die."

"What about the 'two crows for joy'?" Pam asked.

"Well, there are lots of times when something nice is about to happen, when I see two crows. And my mother said there were two crows hanging around when I was born! I saw two crows yesterday." She nodded confidently. "So I guess it means good luck that you all are moving in."

Shelley smiled at her. It was a nice thought.

" 'Three crows a wedding'?" Pam went on.

"Right. Before my mother married my father. That's why her father didn't object; he knew it was fated," Gale said seriously.

"But you weren't a boy."

"There weren't any four crows around when I was born, either!" Gale said. "But there were four crows before Uncle Sol was born, my mother said. So she knew I was going to be a girl because there were only two crows—for joy," she added complacently.

"Your mother seems to have believed all that stuff, anyway," Jason said.

"Don't you believe it?" Gale asked intensely. She stood up, and her green eyes were level with Jason's dark ones. "Because if you don't, there's no use your going on with the search. You won't find that five crows mean silver and six crows mean gold and seven crows the secret, unless you truly believe it. Don't you know that only what you believe is so—*is*? I found that out a long time ago."

"I believe it, Gale!" Shelley said. "We can find what she hid for you. I know we can. Jason, tell her you do believe it. Because we need you to help." She knew she was flattering him; anything boys could do, girls could do as well or better. But the flattery was for a good cause.

"Well, O.K.," Jason said. The strange way Gale was looking at him made him a bit uncomfortable. "So what do we do about the five crows?"

Gale accepted that, Shelley was glad to see; she didn't make him take an oath that he believed it, or anything that wild. "Well, the way I figure it," Gale told them, "is that the five and six crows are signs—symbols, you know—that will show us where the silver and gold that *she* wants me to find are hidden. I don't know what to think about the seven crows," she admitted. " 'A secret that's never been told—' It could be something awful, or she wouldn't have minded telling it." She shivered, though the sun was bright, and Dracula gave a hoarse mutter.

"Maybe not," Shelley said, wanting to comfort Gale. "Maybe it's simply a secret that's never been told till you find the seven crows, and then it can be told. That's probably what she meant. So let's start looking for the five and six and seven crows."

"I've already looked everywhere I can think of," Gale said. "But maybe you all can think of some place I haven't tried."

"Of course it doesn't mean real crows," Jason said thoughtfully. "What we have to look for are five crows that aren't crows exactly. Or are just pictures of crows. Or—stuffed crows? Were there ever any stuffed crows around the old place?" he asked Gale.

"I never saw any," she said. "But of course I've never been up in the attic. I've wanted to go up there, but the nuns have been here ever since I got old enough to think about it. Since they left, I put it off because I don't know how to get into it by my- self. It's over the main part of the house, but there aren't any steps. You can see a couple of little shuttered windows up there, from the outside."

"We'll have to investigate that attic," Shelley said. "It's an obvious place to look. Let's go back to Crauleia and see what we can find."

"Did Mrs. Crawley have the chapel—or was that fixed up by the nuns?" Pam asked.

"It was hers. Of course the nuns liked it and used it for their services, and I guess they put in the statues and Catholic stuff. But my great-great-great-grandmother wanted her own chapel, and she had it fixed up with the stained glass and the pews and all."

"It might be where she hid the something," Shelley mused. "Because a chapel is a special sort of place —that might be why she built it, just to hide the treasure in. Ordinarily, I mean, you wouldn't build yourself a chapel."

"Might be," Gale agreed.

As they came to the old house and followed the path around to the front, Shelley said, "The van's gone! Daddy must have found some men and got the furniture moved in already. He said he could leave the van at a U-Drive-It place in Biloxi. He probably got one of them to take it back over there for him, the way he said he would."

"But whose car is that?" Jason wondered. Another car besides the Calhouns' was parked at the edge of the road that led off the main beach road up to Crauleia, and a man was in it.

"It's Cap'n Boney's," Gale said. "So he got his

boat back in all right this morning, even if there was a storm all night. Wonder what he's doing here?"

"Looks like he's just sitting in his car staring at the place," Shelley said.

"What's eating him?" Jason said. The man in the car didn't look at all friendly, Shelley thought. When Gale waved to him, he didn't wave back. "Well, good thing Dad's back. Mama might be scared if a guy like that came to the door when she was by herself."

"He's not going up to the door at all," Pam said. "He's leaving. He looks mad about something. And he seems to be in a hurry."

The car had started suddenly, taking off at high speed down the road toward Gulf Springs.

"He always drives like that. Crazy." Gale said. "I don't like Cap'n Boney much, even if he is Taz and Raymond's father."

"Then we don't like him either," Shelley said. "Huh, Pam?" Pam nodded.

Bug had run ahead of the others, Dracula flying along with him, and now he grabbed at a piece of paper that was sticking on a spike of the big Spanish bayonet plant that grew in the sand beside the road.

"Watch it, Bug!" Pam warned. "That thing'll stick you and you might get blood poisoning and die!" The plant had long sharp-pointed stiff leaves almost like spears.

"What's that you've got, Bug?" Jason said.

Bug said, "It's some kind of a notice."

"A notice, all right," Shelley said, taking it from
him. "Look! It's a—a threatening letter, I think."

She stared at it—red letters inked large on a piece
of yellow paper, as if with a marker. Or—Shelley
couldn't help thinking—with blood.

"What does it say, Shell?" Bug asked. "You didn't
give me time to read it before you snatched it. You
forgot I don't read very fast."

"Sorry, Bug," Shelley said. "I didn't mean to snatch
it."

"It says—" Pam read slowly over Shelley's shoulder,
"DON'T STAY HERE.
THIS PLACE IS DANGEROUS."

Cap'n Boney's Warning

"You think Cap'n Boney put it there?" Shelley asked Gale.

Gale shrugged. "I told you he's crazy. But I never thought he was that crazy. Why would he care if you stay here or not?"

"Maybe it's just a friendly warning," Pam said doubtfully. "Maybe he heard about the ghosts and just wanted to tell us."

"Well, let's show the note to Daddy," Jason said. "It doesn't sound too friendly to me."

The five rushed in all together. Shelley saw Daddy and Mama in the midst of boxes and furniture, looking hard at work but happy, and she hated to tell them that they were in danger.

"Dad!" Jason said. "Look what somebody left sticking on that Spanish bayonet bush outside. We think it was Cap'n Boney Willis. He was in the car that scratched off just as we came up."

"Who," said Daddy, "is Cap'n Boney Willis?" He took the paper and scanned it. Mama read it too, over his shoulder.

"He has a shrimp boat," Gale said. "He lives over at the trailer park. Two kids." That was about all you could say to tell anybody who Cap'n Boney was.

"Mama," Shelley said, "and Daddy, this is Gale Franklin. We told you about meeting her. Her great-great-great-grandmother built Crauleia."

Mama smiled at Gale. "I'm glad the children have already found someone they like for a friend." Gale smiled back, and murmured hello.

Daddy said absently, "Hello, Gale." Then he told Jason, "This has to be some kid's joke, son. No shrimp boat captain would do such a childish thing."

"Gale thinks he might."

"He's not like most shrimp boat captains," Gale confirmed. "He hardly ever brings in any shrimp to speak of. He hardly catches enough to pay Roscoe's wages."

Daddy shrugged it off. Shelley could see he didn't think Gale knew everything she thought she did. "Somebody's trying to scare you kids, that's all. Just to see if you believe in those ghosts, I guess."

"If you meet Cap'n Boney Willis," Pam said in a sort of scared voice, "will you ask him about it, Uncle Jonathan?"

"I certainly will, Pam."

Mama said, "Are you all ready to help now? We've got the water and electricity turned on at last."

Shelley told Gale, "I guess we'll have to postpone the search till we get the place straightened up a little. But we won't forget. We'll be thinking about what the clues mean. How'll we get in touch with you? I guess we don't have a phone yet."

"I'll be around," Gale said. "But if you just follow the path from the Crows' Roost the other way across the Crows' Wood, you'll come to my house. See you tomorrow, then. 'Bye."

Bug said, "Goodbye, Dracula," and the crow actually croaked, " 'Bye." Or it sounded like that.

"Did you hear him, Mama?" Bug squealed. "He talks to me! He answers when I say something!"

"Good," Mama said. "Now if you all will get to work on your rooms, please— Come again, Gale, when we get straight," she called after Gale, who waved as she ambled off. Dracula flew a zigzag course just above her head.

"I'll put up the groceries first," Jason said, "so I'll know where everything is. Shall I cook dinner tonight, Mama? You'll be so busy," he coaxed.

"O.K.," Mama agreed. "If you want to. But I think Daddy just got necessities at the store this time, Jason. No escargots or French artichokes. Just hamburger-and-potato sort of groceries."

"A real chef can make a gourmet meal out of anything," Jason assured her grandly. "A shepherd's pie, for instance, out of hamburger and potatoes. That is, if I can find all my herbs and spices and stuff that I packed." He began to search among the boxes for one he had labeled "Jason's stuff." "Ah, here it is!" He carried it down the basement steps, and Shelley could hear him whistling as he started working in the kitchen.

"We'll fix your room for you, then, Jason," she called to him. "Pam and I will do yours after ours."

"Thanks, Shell."

"He's already thinking about recipes," Pam said.

"He'd better think about lunch before he gets too involved in dinner," Mama said. She went to the head of the basement steps and called down, "Jason, please scrub the table and shelves and stove first, and check if we have everything we need for some sandwiches and sliced tomatoes for lunch."

"Right, Mom," Jason said. "Where are the table-cloths?"

"Just skip the cloth for right now," Mama said a bit impatiently. "Scrub the table and we'll eat lunch without a cloth. We'll use paper plates and sort of picnic, while we're so busy."

"O.K. for lunch," Jason said. "But not tonight, please, Mom! Tonight we'll have linen and silver and a real dinner! We ought to celebrate our new home. I'll make my chocolate mousse for dessert, if that stove will cooperate. I think we have all the ingredients. If we don't, I'll ride my bike to town and get them."

"Sometimes," Mama said, turning back to Daddy,

"it's a great help to have a gourmet child, and then again—"

"—it's a temptation to swat him." Daddy smiled, though, and Shelley knew he didn't mean it. She wished she could do something special, the way Jason did with his cooking. She had tried, but he wouldn't even let her in the kitchen, most times when he was cooking. She thought that was a little bit unfair, when she was the only girl in the family. Oh, well, maybe if she helped Daddy a lot while he was fixing up the school—maybe he'd like that. (He did praise her when her report card was all A's.)

"Would you like for me to help you when you paint the walls, Daddy?" she asked.

"Well, thank you, Shelley. Maybe you can. But I guess if you'll just help clean the rooms right now, that'd be the biggest help."

Shelley sighed, and the corners of her mouth turned down in spite of herself. "Most of the time, Daddy," she said, "you don't have the slightest idea of all I'm thinking about."

He smiled at her in a funny way. "True, my girl. But then, most of the time you don't have the slightest idea of what I'm thinking, either. So we're even."

Shelley took up the mop and bucket again. "Bring the broom and rags, Pam," she said.

After a long day's work their living quarters were beginning to look more like home, Shelley thought with satisfaction. The familiar furniture and pictures and books in the living room gave her a warm feeling of security even in this strange place. Her own room was snug and crowded as usual. Stuffed animals everywhere—Freddy, her big frog, on the bed; posters on the walls: "This is the first day of the rest of your life," reminding her, the same way it always did; her dried orchid from the prom still pinned on the blue ruffled lampshade; Mike's floppy felt hat hanging on a chair back because it had meant something special when he put it on her head, that time. Pam had the other twin bed, but she hadn't brought much of her stuff along, since she was just visiting. Rover in his bowl was on the table beside Pam's bed, though, and Grandma was curled up in Shelley's rocking chair.

The girls had cleaned Jason's and Bug's room for them, but hadn't unpacked any of their stuff. Boys would just as soon never get things straight, Shelley knew.

Jason came upstairs, a smudge of flour on his nose, and looked in on the girls. "Aren't you going to dress for dinner?" he asked.

"We are dressed," Pam said with emphasis on the "are." "We already took our showers and put on clean shorts and our hang-ten shirts. Who're you expecting, anyhow—the Queen of England or somebody?"

"One's own family is more important than any old Queen," Jason said. "I've made my chocolate mousse for you all. The least you could do is dress up to eat it."

"Sometimes, Jason," Pam said with long-suffering

kindness, "you make me sick. You and your *mouse*."

Jason grinned. "I meant to. But seriously, I've cooked a very fine dinner, and everybody ought to help celebrate our being in our new home—Dad's school."

"Well, our new Dior formals haven't arrived yet," Shelley said. "Let's just cool it, huh, Jason? We'll appreciate your mousse O.K. in our everyday clothes. Maybe better. It's really awfully good," she told Pam.

"I hope he washed his hands before he made it," Pam muttered.

"A French chef never washes his hands," Jason told her loftily. "It'd spoil the flavor of his cooking. You know, like you aren't supposed to wash the wooden salad bowl, just wipe it out, so as to keep it seasoned right. My hands are seasoned, see?"

Shelley said, "He washes, Pam. Mama would make him, if he didn't. He's just trying to be funny."

"Ten minutes," Jason said. "I'll be dressed in ten minutes—and you'd better not be late."

"Want me to set the table?" Shelley offered.

"It's already set, thanks. I'm training Bug," Jason said. "And where is that kid now? He's got to dress too!"

Pam said sarcastically, "Don't make him wear his dinner jacket, please, Jason! It's too hot."

Shelley thought, he doesn't really mean to shut me out. But I'll have to do something else, something great. Just to show him—and Daddy—and all of them.

But all she said was, "Race you to the kitchen, Pam!"

Jason had really outdone himself to celebrate. He had put Mama's biggest linen cloth on the longer table, though it reached only about halfway the length of it; he had set the six places at the end covered by it. He had the silver candlesticks with white candles burning in them in the center of the cloth, at either side of a silver bowl of pink oleanders he had gathered from the yard. He was using the rose china and the good silver. He even put on the salad forks, Shelley noticed. The candlelight left the corners of the long room dark and shadowy; there was only a little pool of light centered on the table. It was sort of spooky.

Pam said mischievously, "Why don't we move the forks to the wrong side, before they come?"

"No," Shelley said. "That would be mean. Jason doesn't deserve to have his table disarranged after he went to all that trouble."

"Well, it was just a thought." Pam gave it up reluctantly.

The others came then, and Mama exclaimed about how pretty the table looked, and Bug bragged, "I did it!" Grandma hopped up on it, to see. Jason agonized, "Grandma, get your tail out of the butter!" as he shooed her off.

After Daddy said grace, Jason brought the salad bowl. "We're having the salad course first," he announced. "On separate salad plates. You serve it,

Dad, and pass them." He stacked the plates at the head of the table. "It's chef's salad, with watercress and anchovies," he informed the family as the plates were passed. "I hope you like it. No, Bug, not that fork—*that* one!"

The main course was the shepherd's pie, lightly browned mashed potatoes atop the chopped beef filling. "I didn't know you really knew how to make it," Mama said, smiling at Jason.

"I didn't," he admitted, "till I looked it up. But I had read about it before." There was broccoli with cheese sauce, too, and hot biscuits. "I made them from scratch," Jason said modestly. "No cans."

While they ate, Shelley said, "Jason, should we tell Daddy and Mama the verse with the clues?"

"Yes," Jason said. "Maybe they'll have some ideas about finding the treasure. I think I can say it."

He did, and Daddy looked astonished. "That," he said, "sounds like something Sol Franklin was muttering when he was delirious in 1969, back at the field hospital, after he was wounded. I went to see him, but he didn't recognize me. He was too near death, poor guy. I thought it was just delirium. But of course, he was remembering those clues you were saying Gale had. Maybe there *is* something to the hidden treasure legend in the Crawley family, after all."

"Oh, there is, Daddy," Shelley assured him earnestly. "And we're going to find it—so Gale's father will sell you the place and you can have your school."

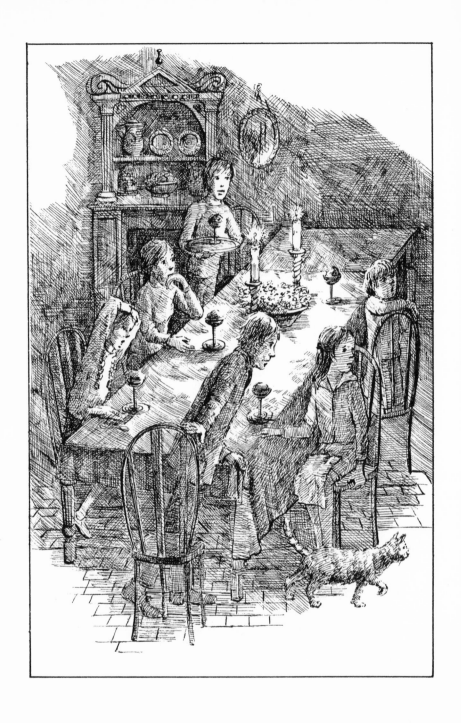

"That'll be great," Daddy said, but Shelley could tell he didn't really believe in it yet. I'll show him, she promised herself.

Just as Jason was serving the chocolate mousse, which had delicate shavings of chocolate atop the whipped cream, Shelley glanced at Pam and saw that her cousin wasn't watching Jason like the rest of them. Pam, who was usually rosy-cheeked, actually looked pale. And scared! She was looking toward the door that opened into the back yard. Her blue eyes were wide and round, and her mouth was open.

"What's the matter, Pam?" she whispered.

"The door—" Pam stammered. "The door! It moved. It's—it's still moving! Somebody's opening the door—"

Shelley looked, and gasped. The light was dim—the candlelight hardly reached that far—but she could see the door. And as she watched, it did move. Slowly, silently, the door was opening.

"Daddy—somebody's coming in!" she cried. "Look —they're opening the door—"

Daddy put down his napkin and went to the door. "Nobody's here," he said, puzzled. "But the door did swing open by itself. Maybe the catch is bad." He examined it and shook his head. Then he went out in the yard and looked around.

"Maybe—whatever it was—came in," Pam whispered to Shelley. "'Maybe it's over there in that dark corner now. Are ghosts invisible?"

"I don't know. They could be." Shelley felt the

prickles go up the back of her neck. She couldn't see anything ghostly, but of course nobody knew all about ghosts. They might be visible sometimes and invisible the rest of the time.

Jason said, "It was probably just the wind that blew it open. Come on back, Dad, and have dessert."

Shelley said, "There isn't any wind."

Daddy confirmed that as he returned to the table. "There's not a breath of air stirring. I wonder how that door came open?"

"Well it wasn't ghosts," Jason said impatiently. "If you all don't eat this mousse right now, I'll never make another dessert as long as I live!"

Daddy hastily took a big bite and murmured appreciatively, "It's great, son."

Bug said, "Please don't stop making desserts, Jason. Stop making salad and that other green stuff, but not desserts."

Shelley said fearfully, "I do want my dessert, Jason. But—didn't you hear—something? Upstairs? I thought I just heard—"

It wasn't stealthy footsteps, exactly. It wasn't banshee howls or clanking chains or anything associated with ghosts. It was just some small noise that was ominous because it was out of place—a sound that had no business being above them at that moment, with no one in the house but themselves.

"Daddy—there's something—" she said.

"I heard something too," he agreed. "I'll go and see who's there."

Bug ate right on, and so did the others, if more slowly. The mousse was really super—even Pam said so to Jason. But Shelley couldn't take another bite till she knew what was upstairs. It could be the ghost. It could be Mrs. Howard Townsend Crawley, come back from the grave, with her familiar, Beelzebub. Or the mysterious old man who had lived and died in the priest's house.

Daddy came back frowning.

"What was it, Daddy?"

He sat down and began to eat his dessert again. "This is a great mousse, Jason," he repeated. "In fact, the whole dinner was excellent. You deserve a *cordon bleu.*"

"Thanks, Dad. But—"

"What was it?" Shelley begged. She swallowed hard. The delicious smooth chocolate cream wouldn't go down her constricted throat. She was scared; she could tell Daddy didn't want them to know.

"Nothing much," Daddy said slowly. He too stopped eating and looked across at Mama. "You didn't leave anything—unusual—in that chapel, did you?" he asked her.

"Why, no. In fact I haven't got around to the chapel yet," Mama said. "I had all I could do fixing up the living room and our bedroom."

"What was in the chapel, Daddy?" Shelley asked, her voice shaky. "*Who* was in the chapel?"

"Nobody. Nobody was anywhere around. But—" Daddy said, "from the hall I could see a flickering sort of light. When I got there, I could see what it was. Two candles were burning on the altar."

"I hope you put them out," Mama said practically. "This dry old building could burn fast if a blaze got started."

"Of course I put them out. But—who lighted them?"

"The ghost?" Pam suggested. "Mrs. Howard Townsend Crawley? She fixed up the chapel, Gale said. She liked it."

"The candles are real enough," Daddy said. He took two white candles out of his pocket and passed them to Mama. They were just like the ones on the table. "Like the ones you buy at the drugstore or grocery. Nothing eerie about these."

"Somebody could have come in, of course," Mama said. "There's a door at each end of the corridor, besides the entrance in the center. And there are the windows, of course."

"But I didn't see anybody." Daddy looked puzzled. "And I thought all the doors were locked."

"The candles are burned halfway down," Shelley pointed out. "They've been burning a while. That is, if they were the same length as the ones on the table. They've been burning nearly as long as we've been at dinner. Somebody could have lighted them as soon as we came down here, and then have gone before you went up there."

"Otto should have barked," Mama said.

"Otto's busy. She's out in the priest's house, having

puppies," Bug volunteered. "At least I think that's what she's doing."

"Why didn't you tell me?" Jason said with irritation. "It's unforgivable for a person to be calmly making a chocolate mousse when a person's best friend is having puppies!" He hurriedly finished his portion and said, "Excuse me, Mama? I need to see about her."

"All right," Mama said. "But don't forget—"

"I'll clean up later," he assured her. One of Mama's good rules, Shelley thought, was the one about anybody could make fudge or cookies or anything they wanted to, but had to clean up the mess afterwards. Though it didn't seem exactly fair, when Jason had cooked the whole dinner for the family, not just something he wanted to eat himself.

"I'll help, Jason," she volunteered as he dashed out the door.

"Thanks, Shell."

He always thanked her. Jason was a good brother, Shelley told herself. She ought not to feel jealous the way she did sometimes.

Bug wanted to be excused too, to go and help Otto have the puppies.

"Let's not," Pam said distastefully to Shelley. "Puppies aren't too cute when they're first born."

"O.K. We'll clear the table," Shelley said.

"Aren't you scared to stay down here?" Pam asked fearfully. "Aunt Susan, are you and Uncle Jonathan going back upstairs?"

"Why, yes, Pam," her aunt said.

"But don't worry. There's nobody out there," her
uncle assured her.

"Nobody we can see," Pam said darkly.

"Mama, do you believe in ghosts?" Shelley asked
as she and Pam started moving the dishes to the sink.

"You'd have to define ghosts before I could answer
that one," Mama said. "What is a ghost?"

"The spirit of someone who's dead?"

"The spirit of someone who's dead may live on in
many ways," Mama said thoughtfully. "But somehow I don't believe in a disembodied spirit that will
waste its time wandering around scaring people by
opening doors and lighting candles."

"There's not much point in it, is there?" Shelley
agreed. "But Gale thinks her great-great-great-grandmother is hanging around trying to help her find the
secret of the seven crows—something the old lady hid
before she died—because Gale is the last of the family
and Mrs. Crawley doesn't want a stranger to find it."

"I hope you'll let Gale find it, then," Mama said. "I
wouldn't want Mrs. Crawley's ghost to think badly
of any of us."

"Oh, we plan to let Gale be first when we find it.
But do you think Mrs. Crawley might not want us
to even help find it, and maybe she—the ghost—is
trying to scare us away by such things as doors mys-
teriously opening, and candles lighted?"

Shelley thought if she could keep Mama talking,
she and Pam might get the dishes finished and not
have to stay down there by themselves.

But Mama said, "Surely not!" and left them to it.

"Hurry, Shelley," Pam said. "It's spooky down here."

"Sure is," Shelley said. "Jason ought to come and help." She went to the back door and called, "Jason!"

Instead of Jason, Bug came running from the priest's house. "It's a great old shack for having puppies in!" he told them. "Otto's having them right in the middle of the priest's bed. It's an old, old iron bed that I guess the vandals didn't think was worth taking. But it's neat. It has knobs on the ends of the bedposts like that one in the movie." Bug's favorite movie was *Bedknobs and Broomsticks*.

"How many puppies?" Shelley asked.

"Two so far. But Jason thinks more are coming. That's why he can't come now."

Shelley said, "Well, tell him to hurry as much as he can, because we're kind of scared of the ghosts."

Nothing else happened, though, while they washed and dried the dishes. The shadows outside the circle of light remained ominous, but you couldn't really hear any strange breathing or sighing, the way you imagined. You couldn't really see an old woman's face mistily appear out of the darkness, though the shadows changed when the girls moved the candles nearer to the sink, and it wasn't hard to see something move with them.

"It's only our imaginations," Shelley told Pam. "I bet people who don't have much imagination never see ghosts. Or hear them."

"Well, if it's not ghosts we hear," Pam said, "Uncle

68 | Jonathan had better set some mouse traps. It might
have been mice—but just now I heard something
that sounded like an old lady in slippers scuffing along
over there by the shelves."

"It's got to be mice," Shelley said, but doubtfully.
She wasn't much fonder of mice than she was of
ghosts. "Hey, Pam—what idiots we are! We could've
turned on the lights. Jason just wanted candles for
the looks of it—we've got lights!"

"Well, we've finished now." Pam looked around
as Shelley snapped on the lights and then turned
them off again.

"Let's go see the puppies, Pam. I'm curious about
them, even if they aren't cute yet."

There were four puppies. "One for each of us,"
Bug said. "This one's mine."

"They won't let us keep them all," Jason told him.
Jason sat uncomfortably on the edge of the bed, with
his hand on Otto's head, just to reassure her that
everything was O.K. The puppies were nuzzling her,
trying to eat.

"Good dog, Otto," Jason said soothingly.

Shelley looked around at the priest's house. It was
spooky, too. Jason had his flashlight-lantern burning;
though there were electric wires here, no bulbs had
yet been put in. There were still some books on a
shelf by the window, books with tattered leather
covers. Probably the vandals didn't care much about
reading. But the old-fashioned iron bedstead, with

the mattress still on it where Otto lay with the pups, was the only piece of furniture left.

Her thoughts kept going back to the mysterious old man who had lived here in Mrs. Howard Townsend Crawley's time and had probably died in this very bed. It looked old enough. It had once been painted white, but was now chipped and rusty. For some reason this old guy seemed more real to Shelley than the Father Bryan named by Gale—the priest who had lived here only two years before and had fled with the nuns from the hurricane. There was a ladder standing in one corner of the room. Shelley thought, I wonder what Father What's-his-name needed with a ladder in his house.

"Can't Otto manage by herself now?" she asked Jason. "Maybe she'd like a little privacy to wash her babies."

"O.K.," he said reluctantly. "I'll do the dishes now. Come on, Bug. The pups will be better off with just their mother. They're going to be great watchdogs *and* hunting dogs, with a mother and father like theirs!"

Shelley and Pam waited for him to be surprised at finding the kitchen all cleaned up. They nudged each other as the four crowded in through the back door and Jason turned on the light.

Jason said, "What a mess!"

Shelley and Pam looked at each other in blank astonishment. That wasn't the reaction they had expected. They pushed past Jason—and then they screamed.

"The ghosts! They've messed up everything. We had it all cleaned up for you, Jason, and now look!"

The clean dishes and silver they had stacked on the shelves and in the drawers were strewn around on the table again haphazardly. The garbage had been dumped out of the can into the middle of the floor. There was ketchup smeared on the stove Jason had cleaned that afternoon, and broken eggs dribbled among the clean dishes.

Bug said, "Wow!" at last.

"Well, at least they didn't break all of Aunt Susan's good dishes," Pam offered uncertainly.

"Mrs. Crawley wasn't crazy—like this," Shelley said slowly. "Gale said she was crazy, but she didn't mean out of her mind. This ghost isn't doing things that make any sense. It couldn't be Mrs. Crawley's ghost."

Jason said to Shelley, his eyes big and seeing more than the scene in front of him. "You and Pam had it all cleaned up when you came out to the priest's house?"

"Yes, we did. And now look! Why would a ghost—?"

"It was a real mean ghost," Bug said.

"Shelley," Jason said solemnly, "This was no ordinary ghost. From what I've read, it could only be one certain kind of ghost."

"What kind?" Pam said fearfully.

"Did you guys ever hear of a poltergeist?"

The Poltergeist Theory

"I think maybe I've heard of it," Shelley said, "but I don't remember much about it. What is it exactly?"

"A poltergeist," Jason said, "—and I'm not even sure that's how to pronounce it—is a mischievous spirit that likes to break things and play tricks and mystify people just for the fun of it. This certainly does look like the work of a poltergeist."

"I'll call Uncle Jonathan," Pam said and ran for the stairs.

Shelley said to Jason, "I'm all over goose bumps. It doesn't fit. There's some sense to Gale's theory about Mrs. Crawley's ghost haunting this house. But no sense at all to a poltergeist haunting it. And Gale didn't mention such a thing in the Crawleys' traditions."

Jason said thoughtfully, "It might have just come.

I mean, when we did. Poltergeists do their haunting in houses where there are teen-agers. I'm a teen-ager, and we could stretch a point and say you and Pam are —at least you're in your thirteenth year. Probably the poltergeist wasn't here before."

"That sounds as though the teen-agers were responsible for the tricks," Shelley said, her voice shaky. "Jason, you don't think—it couldn't be—*us?* You aren't thinking we play tricks when we don't know we're doing it? That's the most frightening thing yet."

"Let's think it through," Jason said. "We were all together at the table when the door opened by itself. So we didn't do that, at least. The candles—well, they had burned down considerably. I suppose it would have been possible for me to have lighted them just before I came down to supper. But the mess in here —I was out in the priest's house with Bug."

"But Pam and I could have done this—if we were being poltergeists together," Shelley said. "Only we didn't! Two people can't lose their minds at the same time and forget what they did—can they?"

"No. But an objective observer could say you planned it to fool the rest of us and are lying about not remembering it. Or that the three of us are doing it together—you and Pam that part and me the candles."

"There's no sense to that theory," Shelley said. "Two of us know we didn't. We don't want to scare anybody; we just want to solve the mystery of the seven crows. Besides, none of us could have made the door open."

"Well," Jason said, "we'll watch each other, Shell. If I'm ever a poltergeist, I want to know it!" Then another thought struck him. "Gale! She's a teen-ager, too. She could have opened the door. And it's possible she could have got in and done the other things, too."

"I don't believe Gale is a poltergeist," Shelley said firmly. "And she'd have no reason for scaring anybody. All she wants is to find out the secret. Like us."

"But maybe poltergeists can't help what they do," Jason argued. "She probably doesn't know it, if she is."

Daddy and Mama came then, with Pam, and looked at the room in dismay.

"I didn't think those vandals would come back after we moved in," Daddy said.

"I wish they hadn't broken anything," Mama said regretfully. "I don't think my china is open stock any more. I probably can't replace it. But they broke only a cup and a salad plate."

"Probably that was an accident," Shelley said. "Maybe they didn't mean to do it. If they're poltergeists, like Jason thinks, they're just mischievous ghosts and don't really mean any harm when they play tricks."

"Poltergeists!" Daddy laughed. "No, nothing as interesting as that. I think it's just a simple case of vandalism. We'll have to be sure all the doors and windows are locked, after this. But I thought at least the doors were locked this time."

"Poltergeists come right through closed doors," Jason said ominously. "Or they can open locked doors. And they can play tricks without even being there."

"It's no poltergeist," Daddy said positively. "There's no such thing."

They finished clearing up the kitchen again, leaving everything put away neatly. This time Mama stayed with them to help. When she called up the stairs to say they had finished, Daddy came back down to be sure the kitchen door was locked securely and the windows fastened down.

"What about the other doors and windows?" Mama said. "All locked? But of course we can keep the bedroom windows open? It's too hot to sleep with closed windows."

"It should be all right to open them upstairs," Daddy said. "I'm glad Mr. Franklin gave me keys to all the doors. Now they're all locked."

"He might have duplicate keys, though," Mama said. "Let's remember to ask him if they're in a safe place where nobody could steal them."

Shelley's mind unwillingly picked on Gale. Gale could have gotten a key to the house.

But Gale wouldn't play such childish tricks. Would she?

As they went upstairs she asked Jason, "Should we tell Gale about the poltergeist?"

"Sure. Maybe she can think of some explanation. Or something to do about it. I'm certain she doesn't want poltergeists around to make it harder for her great-great-great-grandmother's ghost to help us find the secret."

"You're beginning to believe in ghosts, too, aren't you, Jason?" she said wonderingly.

"Not really. But if there even *might* be ghosts, it's no use taking chances. We should go along with the possibility, so as to be on the defensive, see?"

"I guess so," Shelley said. "Anyhow, we'll tell Gale tomorrow, O.K.?"

"Right," Jason said.

Nothing else happened while they were all in the living room watching TV that evening, except that a picture Daddy remembered hanging very securely that afternoon fell off the wall for no reason. Jason said, "See? Poltergeists are always making pictures fall."

"But we were all right here," Shelley whispered to him.

Daddy examined the place where the picture had hung. "The hanger was loose, and just pulled out with the weight of the picture," he said. "But I could have sworn I left it firmly driven in. Somebody could have loosened it, I guess. But there's no earthly reason why anybody would want to."

"How about unearthly?" Shelley said.

"Forget it," Daddy told her. "If you see any ghosts, Shelley, let me know right away. I'd like to see one myself."

When Shelley and Pam were ready for bed, Shelley

found she didn't much want to turn out the light. She was shivering, in spite of the hot weather. "Are you scared?" Pam asked from her bed. "I am. Sort of."

"I guess I must be," Shelley said. She laid her blue blanket across her bed.

Pam had been told about the poltergeist theory, but it didn't trouble her. She said positively that those things had nothing to do with her; she knew everything she did, and she hoped the rest of them did too. But she was going to be just as scared as she liked, of the real ghosts. It was, in fact, kind of fun to be scared, she said. "I wrote Margaret and Elizabeth all about it," she told Shelley with satisfaction. "They've never slept in a haunted house." Margaret and Elizabeth were her older sisters—who usually got to do the things Pam had never done.

"You haven't either—yet," Shelley pointed out as she turned off the light and got in bed. "Maybe we can't sleep at all. Maybe we'll never sleep again! At least not till we get rid of the ghosts."

Pam turned over and pretended to snore, and after a while she was really asleep. Shelley could tell by her breathing. But Shelley lay there in the dark, her body almost rigid with apprehension, staring into the blackness. She didn't know what she was afraid of; that was the worst of it. Was she afraid of a ghost? No —she had always wanted to see a ghost; she would have liked it to answer some questions. Was she afraid of mischievous spirits like poltergeists? They didn't really harm people with their tricks. No—she was simply troubled by the mysterious, the unexplained.

In her mind she wasn't afraid, but her body was all prickles and goose bumps, nevertheless. If only I could solve the secret of the seven crows, she thought, maybe it would clear up everything.

After a while, in spite of her apprehensions, she went uneasily to sleep.

The next morning, when she woke up early and opened her eyes, the sky she could see without leaving her bed was pale like mother-of-pearl, barely tinted with pastel colors. She lay for a moment, getting oriented to a new room, a new window, a new sky scene. Everything was changed from the way her room had been in her old home. Yet she didn't feel homesick; she felt adventurous, if a bit unaccustomed to the changes.

Then she remembered why she felt so keyed up for something to happen. Of course! The secret of the seven crows! How could it have slipped her mind for one moment? She hopped out of bed in a hurry, re-membering how many urgent things there were to do today. Tell Gale about the poltergeist—see the puppies—solve the mystery—

She couldn't believe it when she saw what was hanging across the top of her dressing table, ob-scuring the mirror.

It was the light-blue blanket she remembered get-ting, just before she went to sleep, because thinking about the poltergeist made her feel chilly.

Now who would have put a blanket in such an un-likely place?

Slowly, unwillingly, she faced it. Poltergeists? She

could have done it herself, without knowing it. Or Pam could have. Or Bug or Jason.

But she didn't believe any one of them did.

Then—whoever or whatever was haunting the house had been in her room last night. She gasped, "Pam!"

Pam sat up. "What's the matter with the mirror? What did you cover it up for?"

"I didn't," Shelley said. "It was the poltergeist."

Pam looked scared. "Weird. Crazy." She glanced quickly at the bowl and reported, "Well, at least Rover's safe."

The door to the hall was open again. Now Shelley heard a yell from Jason. "I told you not to ever bother my cookbooks and recipes!" he was shouting at Bug.

Shelley said, "It got into their room, too."

She and Pam hurried to find out what had happened. Jason's cookbooks were all scattered about the room, and loose recipes he had clipped from newspapers and magazines were everywhere.

Bug was protesting, "I never touched them!"

Jason calmed down and apologized. "Sorry, Bug. For a minute I forgot about the poltergeist."

Daddy came then, and he and Jason went to check all the windows and doors again. Of course, they were locked.

"Well," Daddy said to Mama, "it does begin to look very odd. Shall I tell the police?"

"They'd only say it's got to be an inside job," Jason told him. "With all the doors and windows locked from the inside—"

"Or else," Shelley said, "they'd just laugh and say everybody knows this old house is haunted. And they'd advise us to leave. Like that note did."

"Well, I'm not going to leave," Daddy said definitely. "So you all will just have to get used to cleaning up after our houseguests. Some people"— he turned to Mama with a rueful, resigned sort of laugh— "have cockroaches. Some people have termites. We seem to have poltergeists."

"You really believe that, Uncle Jonathan?" Pam asked seriously. She wanted to be told what to believe.

"Not really, Pam. But if our pests have to have a label, that'll do for right now— Who's ready for breakfast?"

Nothing was wrong in the kitchen, and after breakfast they hurried through the usual chores so as to get away to tell Gale all that had happened.

First, though, Jason said, they had to visit Otto and serve her breakfast in bed and see the puppies. Shelley could tell he was halfway dreading that something had happened to them. But the priest's house seemed undisturbed. Otto thumped her tail, but didn't get up to greet them because the four puppies were eating their breakfast.

"If Otto had been on guard in our room," Jason said to Bug, "the poltergeist wouldn't have got in. She wouldn't have even let him in the house, much less upstairs."

"Maybe she'd have caught him," Bug said, "and we'd at least know what one looks like."

"I'm not sure I want to know." Pam shuddered. She

was sitting on the end of the bed, her hands clasped on the iron bedknob, one on top of the other, her chin resting on the top hand. Then she idly twisted her hands. And the bedknob moved.

She noticed it was loose and began turning it without thinking. It seemed to be screwed on, but was easy to unscrew; the threads were old and loose.

The knob came off in her hand. She looked at it and then looked again, in great excitement.

"S-S-Sh-Shelley," she stuttered. "Jason! Look at this thing! It's hollow!

"And—there's something inside it!"

The Mysterious Note

There seemed to be a piece of paper folded over and crammed inside the bedknob. Pam tried to get it out and couldn't. She handed it to Shelley. "See if you can—I'm afraid I might tear it," she said. "And it might be a clue!"

Shelley pried at the scrunched-up paper, first with her fingers, then with a safety pin that had been taking up the slack in her shorts waistband. The paper was hard to get out without tearing it, but at last she had it.

"Wow!" Jason said excitedly. "It looks like some kind of note. Let me see—"

Shelley wasn't about to give it up. She twisted away from him to unfold it. The paper was yellowed and creased, the ink faded. It looked very old.

"Can you read what it says, Shelley?" Pam was looking over her other shoulder.

"I hope so. But the writing's dim. It's dated May 3, 1912. That's over sixty years ago. 'To whom it may concern—' I think it says. Yes, that's it." She read on, hesitating when she had to figure out the almost illegible handwriting. " 'The doctors say I cannot live much longer. The world has not found out my secret, but Mrs. Crawley knows. For letting me stay at Crauleia, she is to have the gold. It is blood money. My conscience would never let me spend it, since it was payment for a death. I am a patriot and have ever been ashamed of letting myself be paid for a patriotic act—the death of a tyrant. Remember March —the Ides of March remember. All the conspirators save only he did what they did in envy of great Caesar. He only, in the general honest thought, and common good to all, made one of them. Night hangs upon mine eyes, my bones would rest. J. W. B.' "

"Wow! What a lot of words," Bug said.

"I think the last part is quotations," Jason said. "It sounds like stuff we had in school. Wonder what it means?"

"Gold!" Shelley snatched the one word out of all the others. " 'Six crows means gold.' So there *is* a treasure, someplace."

"And Gale wouldn't mind spending it," Pam said. "She wouldn't need to have any conscience feeling about it."

"Only you can't spend gold nowadays," Jason remembered. "But probably she could turn it in at a federal bank and get whatever it's worth in money that can be spent."

"Let's go tell her!" Shelley said. "And maybe she knows something else about the old man her great-great-great-grandmother let live in this shack. I'd like to know more about him—like who it was he killed—wouldn't you?"

"Well, the note's sort of like a will," Jason speculated, "telling anybody that found it that Mrs. Crawley was to inherit his gold. But I wonder why he hid the note. Seems to me he would've left it where it could be found after he died."

"Maybe Gale can think of more about it after she reads this," Pam said. "Come on."

Jason patted Otto and each of the puppies; so Bug had to pat them, too. The girls were already on the woods path before the other two caught up with them. They found the path went straight to Gale's house, as she had said. Crows scattered and flew as they approached.

Gale's house was an odd sight. "It's just half a house—it really is," Shelley marvelled. "It looks like a giant took a knife and sliced off half of it." The hurricane had left a ragged edge of inner wall, but the rooms formerly at the back of the house had disappeared. Rubble was still on the ground, but the winds must have carried the larger part of the walls away. Huge fallen trees lay everywhere. "No wonder she wants so bad to find the money to rebuild it."

They called, "Gale!" but nobody came out. Then Pam said, "What are we waiting for anyway? Let's ring the doorbell. After all, there's still a front door."

The others waited at the door while Jason rang.

After what seemed a long time, Gale, with Dracula on her shoulder, opened the door. "Hi," she said. "I was just helping my father dress. He has arthritis, and it's hard for him to lift his arms. But it's O.K. now."

"Come on out to the Crows' Wood," Shelley said, since Gale didn't ask them in. "We've got lots to tell you. And show you."

"Let me tell my father," Gale said.

She came back in a moment, and walked with them into the woods. As they went past the hurricane's havoc at the back of the house, Gale said, "See why I need Great-great-great-grandmother's treasure? We have to crowd everything into the three rooms left. And the roof over them leaks." Shelley thought sympathetically, she can't ask us in because the house doesn't look decent.

"We'll find it," she said, though she wasn't as confident as she sounded. "And there really was some gold! We've found a strange note that old man who lived in the priest's house must have left hidden in the bedknob."

"A note!" Gale exclaimed. "What did it say?"

"You'll have to read it. Wait till we get to the Crows' Roost. Was that old iron bedstead in the priest's house now the one the old man had?"

"I'm sure it was," Gale said. "My mother said Father Bryan used the furniture that was already there; it was there from way back. There were other things, but my father wasn't well enough to keep people from looting, after the hurricane when the nuns left."

"A few of Father Bryan's books are still there," Jason said. "I looked at them. They're in Latin—his *Ritualia Romanum* and some other Catholic-looking books."

"I know," Gale said. "I looked at them but I couldn't read them. Have you had Latin?"

"Only first year. I couldn't read them either—just a word or two sometimes."

"What's a *Ritualia Romanum?*" Pam asked.

Jason told her, "I think it's the formula for all the rites of the Catholic church. Like the sacraments— mass for the dead, and for weddings, and all that stuff."

"Where's the note?" Gale said as they came to the Crows' Roost and sat down on the fallen tree trunks.

"Here." Shelley handed it to her. "Pam just happened to twiddle with the knob and it came off, and this was folded up inside."

Dracula hopped down from Gale's shoulder and began to explore the underbrush. A second crow came out of a nearby pine and joined him.

"Look!" Bug said. "Dracula has a friend. They look like they're talking about something. Just like we are."

"They are," Gale told him.

Jason asked, "And what do you know about poltergeists, Gale? Did Crauleia ever have them—before?"

She paused in unfolding the note. "I never heard of any," she said. "What about them? What do you mean—*before?*"

They all talked at once, telling her what had happened the night before. Gale shook her head. "This is something new," she said. "As far as I ever heard, nothing like that ever happened before. The ghost legends have been weird all these years, but not like that." Shelley thought Gale seemed honestly surprised; she really hadn't had any idea about the mischief-making ghosts. No, it couldn't have been Gale coming in with an extra key her father had, to play those tricks.

After she read the note found in the bedpost knob, Gale said, "This is a case for Mr. Dilmous Wilson! All that poetic stuff—that's just what he knows all about. Let's go and see what he makes of it."

"O.K.," Jason said. He was curious about Mr. Dilmous Wilson. "But it's pretty clear the old man had some gold he was ashamed of, that he wanted to leave to Mrs. Crawley because she was good to him. Probably that was what she wanted to leave to her descendants, when she wrote that about the six crows. She might have had qualms, too, about spending blood money, but maybe she thought *they* wouldn't have any."

"He killed somebody for it," Shelley said. "I don't see how Mr. Dilmous Wilson could ever tell who it was, but it won't hurt to ask him. I wanted to see him feed those sea gulls, anyhow."

"This is just about the time he goes down to the beach," Gale said. "Let's find him."

She gave a peculiar cluck and Dracula flew back to her shoulder. They led the way down to the beach.

"How far is it?" Pam said.

"Not far. He lives just outside of the town. His house was bummed up some by the hurricane, but he fixed it up himself. He was glad all of his books weren't damaged. A few were, though."

They ran along the beach, Dracula flying zigzag alongside. "Does Dracula like sea gulls?" Bug asked.

"No. They fight over the little fish they find in the pools when the tide goes out."

Far down the beach they could see a great flock of sea gulls, fluttering around a solitary figure. The birds lit on the sand and picked up what the man strewed before them.

"What does he feed them?" Pam asked, fascinated.

"All kinds of scraps. They eat anything. Scavengers, that's what they are."

"Look at the tracks on the beach!" Bug said. "If Gale hadn't told us, we'd never have known why so many bird tracks are here."

Gale waved to the old man, who was wearing a sun helmet and faded denims. He took off the helmet in an old-fashioned gesture of courtesy, and waved back. He had white hair long about his ears, and a bald crown, almost like a picture of Benjamin Franklin that Shelley remembered. He even wore silver-rimmed eyeglasses. He held a bucket of scraps he was throwing to the gulls.

Gale made the introductions. "Shelley and Pam and Jason and Bug, this is Mr. Dilmous Wilson. Mr. Dilmous, these are my friends who're staying at

Crauleia. Their father wants to start a school there —remember I told you? And we've got a problem for you to help us with."

Mr. Dilmous smiled and said, "I'd shake hands, but you see I've got gull food on them. I'm glad to meet any of Gale's friends."

They all said, "Hi, Mr. Dilmous." Shelley thought she had never seen any eyes that seemed as kind as his. They were dark gray and soft-looking, almost as if you could touch them and they would feel like velvet.

"Hello, Dracula," Mr. Dilmous said. "Have some of the gulls' breakfast."

As if responding to the invitation, Dracula flew down and snatched a bit of fish from near a sea gull's beak. The gull let out a squawk, but Dracula was safely back on Gale's shoulder. Bug squealed with joy. "I've just got to train me a crow," he said.

"It's not easy," Gale said.

Mr. Dilmous told the birds, "That's all," brushing his hands together to show them. "Now come back to the house with me," he invited the children, "and tell me your problem."

He had a little weather-beaten house, set back from the beach and the road, with wind-bent trees at the back and a few oleanders blooming pink and white by the steps. When they came out of the dazzling sunlight into the gloom inside, it was a while before their eyes adjusted. Then Shelley thought she had never seen so many books. Everywhere they covered shelves and

Jason said. "Let's take a chance—the wind's blowing too hard for gnats or mosquitoes, and we can swat the flies." He put the fly swatter handy beside his chair.

Shelley wondered idly why boys should enjoy swatting flies, as she and Pam took the blue plates from the open shelves to the table. "We really need cabinets," she said. "The china and glass would be safer. And they wouldn't get dusty. The nuns didn't have a very modern kitchen, did they? I bet it was just about the same when Mrs. Howard Townsend Crawley lived here, too."

Supper was a lively meal, full of speculations about the six crows and the seven crows, as well as about the mysterious note that was in the priest's house bed-knob. Daddy and Mama were as puzzled as anybody as to what J. W. B. was trying to tell them by all that poetry, and Daddy too wondered why the note was hidden so carefully when it seemed meant to be read. The children had to explain about Mr. Dilmous Wilson and why they gave him the note to study. Daddy said he'd like to meet him.

"We've got to show him the new clues, and tell him about the five crows clue really meaning silver," Shelley said. "Maybe he'll have an idea about the boxed six crows."

Eating and talking, they had almost forgotten the poltergeists. But just as she said that, they were sharply reminded.

A loud crash made them all turn to look at the

shelves in the corner. It sounded like glasses were being broken.

There was little light over there, but it was obvious that something out of the ordinary had happened. Rushing to the shelves, Jason cried, "Something broke about half a dozen glasses! The good ones, too! There's broken glass all over the place."

"*Now* you know, Jason," Shelley said, feeling a little bit relieved as well as scared, "it wasn't any of us. We were all at the table."

"Right. But I don't see how it could have happened —unless it *was* supernatural."

Everybody had crowded around by now. "Could something have been thrown through the window?" Pam wondered. "That window over the sink is kind of on a line with this shelf of glasses. And with the screen out—"

"But I've looked everywhere here for a rock or something," Jason said. "There's not a sign of anything that could have been thrown. Unless it was another glass? And we'd have noticed something as big as that. Besides, you couldn't throw a glass that far, from outside through a window and across the room. It would have to be something smaller than the glasses but solid enough to break them. But there's simply nothing at all here but the broken glass. It's the sort of mysterious thing poltergeists are famous for, of course."

Mama said to Daddy, "It *is* strange. Don't you think the police ought to be told?"

Jason assured her, "Police are simply no good against poltergeists. But I'm getting to the part of the book now where they do something about them. Maybe there's a way we can get rid of them— Of course, in one place in England the ghosts wouldn't leave till the Borley Rectory was burned to the ground."

"That's not a desirable alternative in this case," Daddy told him.

"What does all that mean, Daddy?" Bug asked.

"It means I don't want this place burned down."

Nothing else happened until after everybody had gone to bed. It wasn't easy to sleep; Shelley kept waking with a start out of nightmare-type dreams that she couldn't remember clearly. Then, after a few hours of quiet, strange noises began. Shelley woke hearing a loud knocking that seemed to be directly over her head, and something hard that was apparently being dragged over the floor above her on the third floor.

"Pam! Wake up!" She sprang up and turned on the light, and shook Pam awake. "How can you sleep? Don't you hear it?"

Pam nodded, but she wouldn't get out of bed until Shelley pulled her out by the feet. Then Shelley ran to the boys' door. "Jason! You hear that noise upstairs?"

Mama and Daddy heard it, too. They came into the hall just as the children did, turning on the light. "Let's go and see what's up there," Daddy said grimly to Jason. "The rest of you stay here." Shelley watched them go, her ears separating the sound of their footsteps on the stairs from the knocking and bumping that continued until they had had time almost to reach the third floor; then it abruptly stopped.

And after a moment the lights went out. Shelley screamed; Pam and Bug did too. Mama automatically said, "Hush!" They huddled together around her, straining their ears and eyes toward the darkness at the top of the stairs. They could hear sounds that Shelley thought must be Daddy's and Jason's footsteps, but these sounds faded away. It seemed like forever, waiting.

"Let's get flashlights and go up there," Shelley said after a while. "Please, Mama? We can't just stay here."

"I know it seems like a long time," Mama told her, "but really it's been only a few minutes. Still, I guess we'd just as well be doing something as waiting. Have you got a flashlight in your room, Shelley?"

"Yes'm. I'll get it."

Bug said, "I know where Jason's is." They came back in a minute, and their two beams of light flashed around the long hall.

"There's somebody—at the other end!" Pam whispered.

The light in Shelley's hand wavered. Then as she saw who it was she breathed a great sigh of relief. "It's Daddy and Jason! They came down the other stairs!"

"What happened?" Mama grabbed Daddy and held onto him hard for a minute. Shelley wanted to do it too but she didn't.

"Nothing. We turned on the light at the top of the stairs. Nobody was there. Before the lights went out we saw the vacant hall and the empty room. There was a big stick on the floor; it could have been used to make the noises we heard. The rooms open into each other but we couldn't see beyond the first one while we had the light."

"In the dark, though, we thought we saw a white misty thing going down the hall!" Jason said. "But we followed it to the other stairs and lost it there. Did you see anything?"

"No, not a thing down here," Mama said. "We were too petrified to look—but we'd have seen it if it had come through the hall in this direction. It probably went on down the next flight."

"It just disappeared," Jason said. Shelley thought he looked as though he believed in ghosts now.

"This place has too many staircases," Pam muttered. "Can't you close them off or something, Uncle Jonathan?"

"We need them in case of fire, Pam," Daddy explained. "If we have students sleeping in third-floor dormitories, we need to be prepared to evacuate them at either end if a fire should start at the other end."

"Fire drills!" Bug said. "We've got to have fire drills."

"Exactly." Daddy nodded.

"But now the poltergeists—or whoever's trying to scare us—can get away too easy," Pam said.

"Ghosts don't need stairs," Jason muttered.

"You don't believe in ghosts," Bug reminded him. "I do and I'm scared."

"I'm beginning to, though," Jason admitted. "All this is too weird."

Shelley was shivering again. She wasn't sure whether she wished she had seen the white shape or not.

Daddy said, "I'll go down and check the doors and windows on the first floor—and in the kitchen. Give me one of the flashlights, please. Go back to bed now, kids."

"I'll come too," Jason said. "But I know they'll be locked. We won't find a thing. Ghosts don't use doors and windows. Neither do poltergeists."

"Let's go to bed," Mama told Shelley and Pam and Bug.

"Let's not," Shelley said. "Not till they come back, please, Mama."

In a few minutes the lights came back on. "Simmer down now," Daddy said when he and Jason returned. "Everything was locked up tight downstairs." He had found a fuse missing from the fuse box and replaced it. "Ghosts don't take out fuses," he said.

"Poltergeists might," Jason said.

"Goodnight," Daddy said firmly. "Everybody back in bed!"

Shelley tried, but she couldn't sleep. Long after Pam was breathing her asleep way, Shelley lay rigid, afraid of something she didn't understand. It was funny, she thought, how everything was scarier at night. You could be brave about lots of things in the daytime. Even ghosts. But at night your skin prickled and you shook till your teeth chattered, when you thought about something supernatural waiting in the dark.

She couldn't stand it any longer. She had to see if Jason was still awake. It was comforting to have an older brother awake too, when you couldn't go to sleep at night.

She pushed open his door softly.

A beam of light struck her in the face. Jason's flashlight pointed at her from his bed, and Jason said sternly, "What are you doing, Shelley, creeping around in the dark? What were you about to do?"

His voice sounded accusing. After a minute Shelley realized why.

"I'm not—I wasn't—going to do anything," she stammered. "I'm not the poltergeist, Jason! Truly I'm not. I was just scared, that's all, and I wanted to see if you were awake."

Jason turned the beam of light away from her, then, and his voice was normal when he spoke. "Well, O.K.," he said gruffly. "I don't blame you for not being able to sleep, Shell. I don't see how Bug can go right to sleep with all this going on. Let's talk low, though, so as not to wake him. All of us were at the table when the glasses shattered—so I know you aren't the poltergeist. Even subconsciously—the way some teen-agers are poltergeists without knowing it—you couldn't pull off a trick like that."

"What are you doing awake?" she asked. "Can't you sleep either?" She crumpled down on the edge of his bed, dejectedly.

Jason sat up and put an arm about her comfortingly. "I've just finished reading that book about poltergeists. And, Shell, I know how to get rid of them!"

"How?" she asked excitedly. "Will it—hurt?" She didn't want—anybody—to get hurt. But of course, she told herself, she *knew* it wasn't Gale.

"I don't think spirits can feel anything," Jason said. "They don't have bodies."

"What are you going to do?"

"Wait till tomorrow night. You'll see! That is, if Mr. Dilmous can tell me what I need to know. It'll be the most exciting thing we ever did. We'll do it at the stroke of midnight. But, Shelley—" he said slowly, "it might be just as well if we don't tell Gale we're going to do anything. O.K.?"

"O.K.," Shelley said reluctantly.

Exorcising the Ghosts

"Don't wake Mama and Daddy," Jason had warned the others before they went to bed. "Sneak down to the chapel at midnight."

It had been a fairly calm day. Gale, when they saw her in the afternoon, had reported that there was indeed a son listed in the family Bible as born to Mrs. Crawley in 1873, when, according to her birth date, she was seventeen. He was named Howard Townsend Crawley, Jr. He had died in 1908. And Gale was certain there must have been a crow perched outside the window when he died, as well as four when he was born.

Jason had been mysterious about what he was going to do that night. He said they'd know soon enough —all except Gale. He had taken an old book out of the priest's house and gone to see Mr. Dilmous in the morning, while Shelley and Pam were helping dust and put up books in the library, and Dad was putting back the painted screens that had dried overnight.

Jason came back in triumph. Mr. Dilmous was just great, he said. But he wouldn't tell them what Mr. Dilmous helped him with—not yet. He did say Mr. Dilmous hadn't had time to figure out the poetic note, though; he was letting his subconscious meditate on what it was all about. The old man thought the new treasure-hunt-type clues were interesting but not very helpful. He didn't have a coin catalog, either. But Gale said her father had written to a coin dealer in New Jersey to ask about the silver dollar.

They had been careful not to let Gale know Jason had gone to see Mr. Dilmous for anything except to tell him about the new clues and ask about any progress on the JWB note. Shelley wished they could let Gale in on it, whatever it was Jason was planning. But Jason said they couldn't yet rule out Gale as "the source of the phenomena," as the book called poltergeist activities. "We're all in the clear, because of the things that happened when we were all together," he reminded Shelley. "After tonight, maybe we'll know if Gale is, too."

"O.K.," Shelley agreed reluctantly. But when they told Gale and Dracula good night, she felt somehow disloyal, all the same. Why, Jason wouldn't even have known Mr. Dilmous if it hadn't been for Gale.

Now Shelley and Pam and Bug crept down to the chapel just before midnight, waiting expectantly for Jason to reveal what he was going to do. They brought flashlights to light their way, but when Jason came he said candles would be better. "This is a ritual," he said solemnly, lighting six white candles on the altar and placing a glass of water beside them.

"What is?" Bug said in a shaky voice. Shelley knew how he felt. She felt the same way. Jason thought he was going to get rid of the poltergeists. Maybe the poltergeists might be figuring on getting rid of *him!* *And* his brother and his sister and his cousin.

"Exorcism!" Jason answered, turning and facing them from where he stood in front of the altar. He was wearing his pajamas—they all were—but Shelley thought he looked a little bit like a priest anyhow (did priests sleep in pajamas like other people?). Jason's big dark eyes were shining with excitement and his expression was solemn and exalted-looking. He didn't act much like a boy who didn't believe in ghosts. "We're going to exorcise the poltergeists. It's the only way to get rid of them, short of burning the whole place down, that book says."

"Exercise 'em?" Bug muttered. "Don't they get enough exercise playing tricks around here and running up and down the stairs?"

"Not that kind of exercise, Bug," Jason explained patiently. "*Exorcise,* spelt with an *o.* The whole thing is in the *Ritualia Romanum*—in Latin. Mr. Dilmous translated it for me. It's great! The only trouble is"— he shook his head a bit doubtfully—"we need some holy water to sprinkle while I say it. I'm afraid it won't work with this plain old tap water."

"Well, if it doesn't work, at least you'll know that's

why," said Pam the skeptic. "It's as good an excuse as any."

"Don't make any noise," Jason warned. "Dad and Mama might wake up and say we couldn't do it."

"Why wouldn't Daddy and Mama want us to do it?" Shelley asked. "They'd surely like to get rid of the poltergeists."

"I just have a feeling they wouldn't like it," Jason said. "They'd say it was either dangerous or sacrilegious or something. Even Mr. Dilmous was doubtful. But he said he was only doubtful that it would work— because it's supposed to be done by a priest noted for his holiness."

Shelley couldn't help giggling, in spite of the cold feeling in the pit of her stomach. No, Jason wasn't exactly noted for his holiness.

"Do the poltergeists have to be here when you do it?" Pam asked him. "Because so far they aren't."

"They're somewhere in the house," Jason said confidently. "Like they live in the walls or something—"

"Like cockroaches?" Bug said.

"The idea is to get them out of the house," Jason went on. "Yes, it'll even get cockroaches, Bug! The ritual is called a '*deprecatoria*'—Mr. Dilmous said that's the same thing as exorcism. It's supposed to rid a house of 'vermin, pests, locusts, and any other kind or animalia.' I asked him if ghosts could be called *animalia*. He said they certainly aren't inanimate— they're in the same general category as devils and angels."

He saw Grandma wander in, and said, "Maybe she oughtn't to be in the house when we do this. We don't want to exorcise Grandma. It might make her run away and we'd never see her again. I'm glad Otto and the pups are outside."

"I'll put her out." Shelley took Grandma to the nearest door, by flashlight, and shoved her outside gently with her foot.

"Well, I'm not scared Rover will leave," Pam said. "He can't get out of his bowl."

"All right, now," Jason said seriously, going to stand behind the altar. "Everybody keep very quiet. Remember this is a solemn sort of ceremony. Mr. Dilmous says you intone it while sprinkling the water, and you make the sign of the cross every time any name in the Trinity is pronounced. I'll be sure to do that—but maybe it won't hurt if you all make the sign of the cross too."

"What's the sign of the cross?" Bug asked. Shelley showed him.

"You watch Jason and do it when he does," she told him.

"What's *that?*"

Suddenly the knocking they had heard the night before began again—but this time it seemed to come from below, from the kitchen.

"They're down there!" Jason said. "It ought to work if we do it right now—" He took a paper from his pocket. The candles started to flicker just as he laid the paper on the altar where he could see to read while using his hands for sprinkling the water and making the sign of the cross. He started to read, in as deep and serious a voice as he could manage, sprinkling water from the glass in his left hand and crossing himself as he came to the appropriate names: " 'I exorcise you, through God the Father and Jesus Christ His only Son and through the Holy Spirit, that you immediately go forth, withdraw promptly from this place, abide here no longer—' "

His voice cracked and sounded too high for the solemn words. Shelley thought, Jason would make a good priest—when his voice gets through changing. The candlelight made strange shadows. How could the candles flicker when there was no breeze inside the chapel? Perhaps Jason's arm, when he raised it to point dramatically at the door, had made the air move a little? Or when they all made the sign of the cross, was the motion enough to waver a candle flame?

Jason cleared his throat and went on, " '—weakening, decreasing in power so that you cannot harm anyone here; that your remains be not found in this place. I drive you out, *whatever you are!* And may this be done and realized through Him who will come to judge the living and the dead and the world by fire.' "

There was an awed silence after Jason stopped speaking.

After a moment Shelley said, "That's a powerful curse, all right—"

Jason said, "It's better in Latin. Mr. Dilmous read it to me."

"But it didn't work!" Pam pointed out. The noise downstairs hadn't stopped.

Just then they heard rapid footsteps coming down the stairs and rushing on down the next flight to the kitchen.

"Dad heard them!" Jason said.

"He's going to exorcise them, I bet," Pam giggled.

"Come on!" Shelley dashed for the door. They followed her out of the chapel and down the stairs, tumbling over each other in their hurry to get to the kitchen. But Jason remembered to blow out the candles as he left.

Just as they arrived at the foot of the stairs, Daddy turned on the light. They stood blinking at him and at the open back door. Mama hurried down the stairs behind them.

Then into the light from outside came Gale Franklin, her crow clinging to her shoulder, holding a small boy by the arm with each of her firm hands and urging another boy and a girl to go in front of them through the door. "Go on in there!" she was saying to them sternly. "You heard me. You, Patricia! You, Michael!" The two black kids, who looked to Shelley about eight and nine years old, hung back, trying each to get behind the other, but they finally obeyed her.

Shelley thought, so this is what poltergeists look like! And they're not teen-agers at all.

The other two were about nine and eleven, with soot rubbed on their faces, probably so they wouldn't show up white in the dark, until they got ready to "appear" as the ghost at the end of the hall, Shelley surmised. And how did they do that?

Gale released the two she was holding, and said to Shelley, "What have they been up to? I caught them running out of the kitchen door."

"I guess they were making all the noise we heard down here," Shelley answered.

"I guess," Jason said slowly, as if reluctant now to give up the idea of anything supernatural existing, "I guess they're the poltergeists. But how—? They don't look smart enough to fool us with all those tricks. How did they make the glasses break, for instance?"

"Well, how did you?" Gale said. "Come on, Taz, you can tell me! Raymond, give!" Dracula croaked, three syllables that sounded like, "You'd better!" Bug held out his finger and Dracula hopped onto it. Bug stroked his feathers, fascinated. He cared more about trained crows than poltergeists, that was sure.

The Willis boys shook their heads stubbornly. They weren't saying a word. Michael and Patricia followed their lead and kept quiet, too.

Shelley saw Daddy's lips twitch, as if he were trying to keep from laughing. She knew the four kids could never be scared Daddy would hurt them. So probably they'd never let on how they did the tricks. Too bad.

Daddy said to Gale, "Looks like they aren't even going to give us their name, rank, and serial number. That's all a soldier in the army is required to tell when he's captured by the enemy."

"Their names," Gale said, "are Taz and Raymond Willis—these two. Taz is the one with the slingshot hanging out of his pocket. And those are Patricia and Michael Lummus. They're friends of mine—or rather, they used to be," she emphasized, looking at them significantly. "If they'd confess what they were up to, we could still be friends." She frowned at Taz, who looked the oldest. "Come on, Taz. What were you doing here? And why?"

Still the boy shook his head. He looked so ridiculous with his face and hands blacked and even his tow-head streaked with soot, that Shelley could see why Daddy was about to break up. It was funny. Even Mama was having a hard time not laughing. Yet it was her china and glassware they had broken. And it was sort of serious to let kids get away with vandalism like that.

"They're Cap'n Boney's kids, I guess?" Pam asked Gale.

"Yes, these two are, and Michael and Patricia are Roscoe's. You know. Roscoe is Cap'n Boney's deck hand I told you about."

Dad said, "I suppose I'll have to hunt up Cap'n Boney and have a talk with him. I've been meaning to, anyway, about that warning note Bug found on the Spanish bayonet. So we'll let them go, Gale. I'll speak to their parents in the morning."

Gale said to the culprits, "If you'd come clean, maybe Mr. Calhoun wouldn't tell on you. Maybe Jason and Shelley and Pam and Bug would be your friends, too. How about it? You can have until tomorrow morning to think it over. Can't they, Mr. Calhoun?"

"It would have to be a pretty good story," Daddy said, but he didn't look too severe. "I don't see how they can be let off completely. Unless they had a mighty good reason for all this foolishness."

Michael and Patricia and Raymond all looked at Taz hopefully; he was the oldest. But Taz still wasn't talking. He kept his mouth obstinately shut, and his chin jutted out in determination as he shook his head at the others.

"Think about it," Gale said as she gestured toward the door with her head, in release. The kids scrambled out the door like a bunch of kittens when somebody says scat.

"That was great work, catching them, Gale," Shelley said. "Jason had just finished exorcising them, when you grabbed them."

"Exorcising them?" Daddy and Gale said at the same time.

"Yes," Jason said somewhat ruefully. "Mr. Dilmous Wilson translated the ritual for me, out of the priest's book. But if the poltergeists were only those kids, it was all wasted. And it was such a great curse, Dad! If there *had* been any evil spirits in this house, they'd have had to split."

"Or even any cockroaches," Bug said. "I hope Grandma will come back."

"Hey, you didn't exorcise my great-great-great-grandmother, did you?" Gale said anxiously. "The place won't be the same without her."

"And we may need her yet," Shelley said, "to help us find the rest of the secret of the seven crows."

"I don't know," Jason admitted. "It might have included Mrs. Crawley, for all I know. We'll ask Mr. Dilmous." He brightened up a little, at the idea that his exorcism might not have been entirely futile after all.

A thought struck Shelley. "Gale, how did you happen to be right here on the spot, to catch those kids—at midnight?"

"I often walk around pretty late," Gale said. "Dracula likes to be out at night to see his friends, and of course I don't like for him to go by himself to the Crows' Roost. Something might happen to him—and where would I be if he didn't come back? So sometimes I take him over there to meet his friends, like when they're having a council meeting or something. I told you about how they do it. Well, tonight we walked on over this way—you know, just thinking about the clues and wondering about Mrs. Howard Townsend Crawley and how mysterious she was—and about the old man who lived in the priest's house—and then I thought I saw a light behind the stained-glass window of the chapel. So I was going to investigate, when the kids ran out of the basement door."

"It's pretty obvious they were trying to frighten

you children," Mama said. "But I can't imagine why. It's as inexplicable as that silly note about being in danger here."

"Never mind," Daddy said. "Their father will make them explain it all, I feel sure. Goodnight, Gale. You're going right home, aren't you? Shall I go with you?" Shelley could see he thought Gale shouldn't be out by herself so late at night, but since it was a regular habit of hers, this one time wouldn't make much difference.

"No, thanks, sir. I'm going right home. You needn't worry," Gale said. "Dracula takes care of me. Come on, Dracula. Good night, you all."

" 'Night," they told her, and Bug said a special "Good night, Dracula," as the crow hopped from his shoulder to Gale's. Dracula answered with his usual caw-caw that sounded like goodbye.

Mama said, "We'll all have to sleep late tomorrow, to make up for losing so much sleep tonight."

As they went back upstairs, Shelley said to Daddy, "Can we go with you to see Cap'n Boney tomorrow? I'm curious about that man."

"I don't think we'd better all go," Daddy said.

Shelley felt like crying. He hadn't said he'd take Jason, but of course that was the way it would be. She went to bed but lay awake a long time, feeling hurt and sore inside in spite of trying not to, planning desperately to find the gold—and the secret that had never been told—so that she could give Daddy his wish about buying the place, and maybe then he'd let her go with him when she asked him first . . .

But Daddy didn't take Jason to see Cap'n Boney next morning, after all.

Before they finished their late breakfast, which was more nearly like brunch, Gale came running, Dracula zigzagging in flight along with her. Gale's face was pale and smeared with tears, and her eyes were horrified, as she pulled open the kitchen screen and came in without even knocking. Dracula was caught outside, till Bug opened the screen and let him in.

"Something awful has happened!" Gale panted. "Oh, it's terrible—" And she started crying again.

The Strange Man

"Is it your father?" Daddy said quickly. "Do you need for me to get a doctor, Gale?"

"No, sir—there's nothing anybody can do. Not my father—Taz and Raymond's father. Cap'n Boney— got killed last night—"

Shelley felt a big knock in her chest. Their father was—*dead*. That meant—never again alive. Never to smile or frown again—or hug a child or ruffle his hair— Those two kids. She had to go and put her arm around Daddy's neck, where he still sat at the table, just to hold onto him. What if it were her father? And she hadn't yet had a chance to make him realize how much she loved him.

"What happened?" Daddy asked Gale. "Sit down and tell us, child."

Mama brought Gale a glass of milk, and stood there

smoothing Gale's wild hair back gently while the girl took a gulp of the milk and dabbed at her eyes with Bug's napkin, which was handiest.

"He always drove his car like he had to be there day before yesterday," Gale said then. "So he hit a tree, that's all. Over on Route 90. When I went to the trailer park this morning, Michael and Patricia told me. Taz and Raymond weren't there. Somebody had come and got them last night after they got back from here, to take them to the hospital to see him. But he was already dead, Mrs. Lummus said. She called the hospital but nobody there could tell her where the boys are. Just that relatives had them. Oh, poor Taz, and poor Raymond!"

"I wish," Jason said painfully, "I wish it hadn't been last night we caught them. I wish we hadn't made them afraid something bad would happen to them for being here—at the same time their father was—dying. They're just kids—"

"I don't think they were really afraid," Shelley said. "Nobody could be really afraid of Daddy." She tightened her arm around his neck. He patted her hand absently, before he stood up, shaking her off.

"If there were anything we could do," he said, "we would. But if the relatives are already here I suppose the boys are being taken care of. When I go over to the town I'll ask at the funeral home, though."

"Can I go too, Daddy?" Shelley said forlornly.

"Well, I guess so," Daddy said. "All of you come, if you want to. I'm just going to town and back, to get some nails and paint I need." It seemed to Shelley that he must mean, if she were coming, the rest might as well come too. Do I bug him, she wondered, by always asking if I can do something with him? I guess I do.

"I can't," Gale said. "I've got to go help my father. I haven't even fixed him anything to eat yet. I went over to the trailer park early, before he was awake, to see if—if the kids wouldn't come clean about all that stuff last night. I thought maybe they'd tell me if you all weren't around. And now—"

"Now it doesn't seem so important," Daddy agreed soberly. "I'll put off talking to Michael and Patricia's parents, I guess."

Gale and Dracula said goodbye, and the others got in the car to wait while Daddy asked Mama if she wanted anything from the store.

"Get some limes, please, Mama," Jason suggested, "and I'll make a Key lime pie."

"Some limes, then," Mama said to Daddy, smiling at Jason as she stood beside the car. "I don't believe we need anything else, do we, Jason?"

"I guess we already have the other stuff," Jason agreed. Shelley thought, how can he even think about Key lime pie when that man is dead and those two kids don't have a father any more?

After Daddy bought the things at the hardware store and the limes at the fruit stand, he stopped at the funeral home. The kids waited in the car, subdued by the solemn look of the place. It had great dark magnolias in the front yard, and a sign with "A. B. Mitchell, Mortuary," on it. A hearse was parked on the crushed-oyster-shell drive.

Daddy came back to say, "He'll be taken upstate to be buried, where his family came from. All Mr. Mitchell knows about the boys is that their relatives are taking care of them."

Just then they saw a big car coming up the drive, crunching on the oyster shells. Two ladies and a man were in it, with Taz and Raymond. The car stopped behind the hearse, and Taz got out and came running over to their car. He was all slicked up; there wasn't a bit of soot in his hair; and he had on what looked like a brand-new suit. Shelley knew he had been crying a lot, by the way his eyes were rubbed desperately red. She couldn't think what to say to him, except, "We're sorry, Taz."

He said hurtingly, "I guess—you know what happened to my Dad?"

"Yes. We're sorry, son," Daddy said, and his voice was very kind.

Jason said gruffly, "Sorry, Taz."

But Bug asked, "Are you going to tell us now what you were doing in our house last night? Are you going to come clean?"

Taz looked just plain pitiful, Shelley thought, his chin quivering and his mouth working and tears again in his eyes. "Hush, Bug," Pam said. "It doesn't matter now."

"I—can't," Taz said at last. "He wouldn't want me to. He was a *good* father!" he cried out as if somebody

had denied it. "I don't know why we—and now he
can't ever tell me why he told us to— But he was a
good father. He gave me and Raymond a dollar
every Saturday to spend any way we wanted to. I
was saving up for a bike but he gave us each one for
Christmas. And now he isn't alive any more—he's
not in *there*"— his towhead jerked toward the funeral
home and the dreaded coffin—"he's not anywhere—"
His voice sounded almost unbelieving, the fact was
so hard to comprehend. "And we have to go and live
at our grandmother's. Not even Grandma Willis's.
Grandma Pike's. She didn't even like Dad—but she
came just to get us."

He smeared his hand across his eyes. "Why I came
over here when I saw you—" He looked hopefully
from one to the other of the four children, and at last
his blurred blue gaze came to rest on Shelley as the
most sympathetic—"I wanted to ask you to please
tell Gale goodbye for me. My aunt and grandmother
and uncle don't have time for me to tell her. They're
trying to get us away before my Dad's people can
take us. Gale was my friend—and I guess I won't
ever see her again." He ended with a choking sob
and turned, before Shelley could answer, and ran back
to the car where his relatives waited.

"I will, Taz!" she called after him. "I'll tell her!"
She felt sadder than she had ever felt before in her life.
She hadn't come this close to death before. And she
had never felt so sorry for anybody in her life as she
was for Taz.

But their sympathy for the Willis boys didn't keep

the family from speculating, while they drove home, about why the four kids had been playing ghost tricks in Crauleia.

Pam said, "You know, from what Taz said it seemed like his father was making them do it. He said, 'He wouldn't want me to' when Bug asked him at the funeral home there, to come clean. And he said, 'And now he can't ever tell me why—' So he really doesn't know why Cap'n Boney wanted us scared out of the house."

Shelley said excitedly, "I bet this is why: I bet Cap'n Boney found Gale's secret treasure while the house was vacant—or was about to find it and knew just where to look—but he didn't have time to get it out of the house before we moved in. Remember, that night we came he was out on the shrimp boat in the storm all night, and we were already in the house the next day before he got there. That was when he drove to Crauleia in his car—to get it—and Mama and Dad were there. So the only thing he could figure to do right then was write that silly note. And later he told the kids how to try to scare us. I knew they couldn't think of all those tricks by themselves. That explains it all."

"Except where is the treasure?" Jason said glumly. " 'Six crows are boxed—look for seven crows behind six crows—' What does it *mean?*"

When they got home, Mama said Gale had been looking for them, and she was waiting out in the priest's house with Otto and the puppies. "And,"

Mama told Daddy, "I saw a strange man out there looking in at the door. Otto barked, and I went to the window and asked, 'What do you want?' and he said he just wanted a drink of water. I hated to refuse anybody a drink of water; so I handed him a glass when he came over to the kitchen door—without opening the door very far. He didn't look like the kind of man you'd want in your kitchen. He wasn't very clean, and he hadn't shaved, and he had a sneaky look. I told him just to leave the glass anywhere—that I was busy. And I locked the door and left him there drinking the water. I kept an eye on him through the window until he left, because Gale was out there. He put the glass on the doorstep and went off down the road. But he looked back several times."

"Always keep the doors locked," Daddy told them all. "Even in the daytime. This is such a big house, if anyone got in unobserved he might hide here for a good while before we caught up with him." They all promised.

"Did Grandma come home?" Bug asked. "We put her out before Jason said that stuff last night, and I haven't seen her since."

"Yes, she was here waiting for breakfast," Mama told him. "She's around somewhere."

"I hope Mrs. Howard Townsend Crawley came back too," Shelley said. "We didn't mean to exorcise her—only the poltergeists."

"Probably she never left," Jason said gloomily. "Obviously the exorcism wouldn't work. Because we only had tap water instead of holy water. It didn't matter, because they weren't real poltergeists anyway."

They found Gale sitting on the bed with Otto and the pups, watching them as the puppies nursed greedily. Dracula was trying to drag out another of the small shiny boxes that he had found under some trash in a corner. Bug helped him get it.

"Hey, did you see the man who was hanging around here?" Gale asked them. "He came to the door and looked in, like he was looking for something or somebody, and I was thinking he might grab me and I was planning where to kick him—and then your mother called and asked what he wanted, so he backed out. I thought I'd seen him somewhere before. He looked so sinister, you'd remember him, all right. I've been sitting here trying to remember where it was."

"Well, did you remember?" Pam broke in impatiently. "Where was it?"

"I've just remembered," Gale said tolerantly. "I saw him once with Cap'n Boney at their trailer, that's where!"

"That fits in with my theory!" Shelley said. She told Gale her guess that Cap'n Boney might know where the treasure was, in the house. "And probably now that this guy's heard Cap'n Boney's dead, he wants to get at it himself. Maybe they were in it together and both of them knew—"

"But Cap'n Boney must have double-crossed him," Gale said, "because this guy was looking for it in the priest's house. Or maybe Cap'n Boney hadn't actually told him yet the exact location and he has to hunt around for it just like we do."

"We'll keep a sharp lookout for him," Jason said. "We won't let him get away with anything!"

"And we'll ask Michael and Patricia if they know anything about him," Gale said. "Now that Taz and Raymond are gone, I bet I can get it all out of those two kids."

"That reminds me," Shelley said. She gave Gale Taz's message.

"He wasn't a bad kid," Gale said soberly, not letting any tears show, but sounding as if she could have cried if she'd been by herself. "I didn't like Cap'n Boney, but Taz and Raymond did, so I guess he was good to them, anyhow. He couldn't have been all bad."

"Nobody's all bad," Jason said. "Nearly everybody has something decent about him. And some bad stuff too. Nobody's all good, either."

"I guess he loved one of them just as much as he did the other," Shelley said wistfully. "Taz said he gave them a dollar a week apiece and bought them bikes for Christmas— I hope they got to take the bikes with them to their Grandma's."

"I wish I'd had a chance to tell them goodbye," Gale said. "I wish I hadn't been so hard on them last night. They're just little kids, and I know I'll forget them pretty quick—but it was kind of sad, what Taz said about never seeing me again— Well, I've got to fix Dad's lunch. After lunch, let's go see if we can get Michael and Patricia to come clean." Dracula took the small shiny box in his beak to carry off with him.

"I wonder where those little boxes came from?" Bug said. "Or what they're for. They're even too little for aspirin boxes."

When the group reached the trailer park that afternoon, the Lummus children were playing in front of their trailer, taking turns swinging in the tire swing that hung from a big live oak tree under dripping graybeard moss. Bug said, "Hey, can I have a turn?" and Michael said, "Sure. Let him have your turn, Patricia."

Patricia turned the swing over to Bug and came to ask Gale, "What happened to Taz and Raymond? Some people came and got some things out and locked up their trailer."

"Their bikes too?" Shelley said hopefully.

"I don't know," Patricia said.

"We'll probably never see them again," Gale told her. "That's what Taz told Shelley. They have to go live with their grandmother, up in some place a long way from here. So—" she said sternly, "I want you two to tell me, now, what the four of you were doing at Crauleia—and *why*. Cap'n Boney can't do anything to you now if you tell."

"He could haunt us," Patricia said, round-eyed.

"No, he couldn't. And Taz and Raymond won't ever know it if you tell us. So come on!"

"I'll give you something if you will," Jason promised. He had read about the famous Dr. Skinner's reward-instead-of-punishment system of handling children.

"What? What'll you give us?"

"A dollar to split between you."

"Cap'n Boney gave us each five dollars."

"He did?" Shelley exclaimed.

"For what?" Pam added.

Jason said, "So then you'll have five-fifty apiece, if you tell us all about it."

"And if you don't," Gale said, "Dracula and I won't ever speak to you again, and we'll tell all the crows you're not our friends any more." Dracula, on her shoulder, bobbed his head and gave an affirmative caw.

Bug said admiringly, "I've just got to train me a crow like Dracula."

"Well, O.K.," Michael said. Shelley figured he'd been dying to tell what he knew, anyway, just to feel important about knowing something they didn't. He looked at Patricia, and she shrugged and said, "Might as well. Like Gale says, it can't make much difference now."

"Let's sit down, if it's a long story," Jason said. There wasn't any grass to sit on under the tree where the swing hung, but some of the trees the hurricane had felled were lying nearby, just as they had been left piled and twisted by the great wind. They were fine to sit on, if you cleared the Spanish moss away so you wouldn't get redbugs. Those little red chiggers seemed to like moss better than any place else to live.

Bug found a high, now-horizontal limb that was pliant, so that it bounced him up and down when he rode it astride. "Hey, I've got a horse!" he said. "Come on, Patricia, get you one like this." She followed him bounce for bounce, but the others sat on the solid trunks of the trees.

Michael began, "Cap'n Boney wanted you"—he looked at Jason—"out of that big old house. He gave us five dollars apiece to play tricks that he thought would scare you and make you leave."

"But why did he want us to leave?" Pam asked. "Had he found—?"

"I don't know. But I guess it was 'cause he had some stuff hid in the attic that he wanted to get out, and you moved in while he was away and he couldn't get it."

"The attic!" Jason said, annoyed with himself for forgetting. "We were going to check the attic for Mrs. Crawley's secret—"

"Like I said, maybe he'd found it," Shelley said.

Gale asked Michael, "How do you know he had stuff in the attic?"

" 'Cause Patricia and I spied on him when he was putting it up there. He had the stuff in the house out back first, and then he got Pop to help him move it. A machine thing and some boxes. I think he was trying to put it somewhere else so Mr. Dolph wouldn't know where it was."

"Who's Mr. Dolph?"

"He hung around with Cap'n Boney."

Patricia said from where she was bouncing on her limb, "They were in business together. That's what Pop told me when I asked him."

"So," Jason said, "he's the guy who was here, looking in the priest's house. Maybe he hasn't realized the stuff was moved—whatever it was. I don't see how it could be the treasure, though," he said to Shelley, "or Cap'n Boney'd just have taken it home with him. Unless it's mighty heavy."

"How did he get in the attic?" Shelley asked. "We haven't found the stairs to it yet—or any way to get any higher than the third floor rooms."

"I know where the hole—the trap-door thing—is," Gale said. "Up in one of the closets on the third floor."

"He used the ladder," Michael said. "He kept it in the house out back."

"Then we can use it too!" Shelley said. "Come on! We can get up there ourselves."

"Wait a minute!" Jason said. "I want to know how you kids did all those poltergeist tricks."

Patricia giggled and said, "What'd you call 'em?"

Michael grinned. "That'll cost you another buck," he said tentatively to Jason. "They're pretty good tricks. That Cap'n Boney is a smart man."

"Was," corrected Gale. "So you tell us, Michael, or—" She scowled at him. Shelley realized that sometimes a vague threat was better than a definite one.

"If what you tell us is worth it," Jason said, "I'll give you each another half. But you'll have to wait till I can borrow it from Dad."

Michael said, "What do you want to know? We could get in your house any time we wanted—Cap'n Boney had a key made to the kitchen door, using some kind of wax he mashed onto the lock. He got us black shirts to wear, and he made Taz and Raymond black their faces so they would be black too and not show in the dark. But we had stuff on the other side of the shirts that would shine in the dark. We could whip off the shirts and turn 'em inside out and run down the hall before you could catch us, and we looked like ghosts, with that stuff shinin' like lightnin' bugs. It was easy—with steps at both ends it wasn't hard to dodge you. It wasn't hard to open the back door that first night, either, and get away so you thought nobody'd been there. And to light the candles, of course. Cap'n Boney made the lights go out by takin' out a fuse, after we made the funny noises."

"You didn't have to break Aunt Susan's good china and mess up the kitchen that way," Pam said, frowning.

"Sorry about that," Michael said. "We didn't mean to break the china. But we were in a hurry, I guess, and it got in the way."

"You made the picture fall just by loosening the nail while nobody was around," Jason said, "and leaving it barely hanging there so the slightest jolt would dislodge it. And you could slip into our rooms in the dark while we were asleep. You could make all those strange noises pretty easy, and messing up rooms was nothing. But what I don't understand is how you could make all those glasses on the shelves break by themselves. I know the window was open and the screen was out, but you couldn't have thrown a rock or anything, or we'd have found it."

Patricia giggled again and Michael said, "Is it worth a quarter more, for me to tell you how?"

"Don't give him another cent, Jason," Gale said. "He's going to tell us anyhow." She frowned at Michael and he grinned back.

"Well, O.K. I guess the reason you couldn't find what broke 'em is that it melted. Remember how hot it was that night?"

"Ice cubes!" Pam cried. "I remember now, when we cleaned up afterwards, there was a wet spot on the shelf. We missed seeing the ice among the pieces of broken glass all over the place."

"Taz shot it through the window with his slingshot," Michael said cheerfully. "That guy's a champion with a slingshot."

"Maybe these two ought to have to pay for the glasses and china they broke," Pam suggested.

"Taz broke 'em," Patricia said quickly.

"Well, let's go and see if what Michael and Patricia told us about the attic is true," Jason said. "Maybe we'll let them off, since they've turned state's evidence. If there's really something significant in the attic and it proves they're telling the truth. Come on, let's go investigate that right now."

Dracula came to Bug of his own accord and rode on Bug's shoulder all the way back to Crauleia. Bug muttered, "I've just got to—"

Pam said, "We know. You've just *got* to train you a crow like Dracula."

There was a note from Mama and Dad on the hall bulletin board where the family always left messages for each other. "Gone to town. Will be back in a couple of hours. If not home by six, will Jason please start something for dinner?"

"Good thing they had us our own keys made," Pam said, "or we couldn't have got in to read the note."

"Maybe I'll have time for the attic search before I start dinner, though," Jason said. "Let's hurry and get the ladder."

It wasn't easy to carry it up all those stairs, and Shelley wondered why Cap'n Boney didn't just leave it up there.

"Because it would give it away," Jason said. "In the priest's house, we never thought of the ladder as being there because he had something way off here in the attic. If it had been up here on the third floor, though, we might have guessed."

"This is so exciting!" Pam said. "Elizabeth and Margaret don't know how much fun I'm having! I'm going to write them another letter tonight."

"If we find anything worth writing about," Gale said gloomily. "I'm afraid Shelley's idea about Cap'n Boney's knowing where the gold is couldn't be right. So if anything's up here, it probably isn't the secret."

"Well, we're going to look," Jason said with determination. "So show us the trap door."

Gale led the way to the closet, Michael and Patricia agreeing that this was the part of the house they had

followed Cap'n Boney and their father to. "They
went right up that ladder and pushed that board
thing over the hole to one side, and climbed up into
the attic," Michael volunteered. "Had a hard time
gettin' that machine thing up there, though. It was
as big as a TV set. They had a lot of other stuff, too."

"The stuff better be there now," Gale said ominously. "You wouldn't lie to us, would you, Michael?"

"Cross my heart it's the truth!" Michael said.
"Cross my heart, Gale. I wouldn't lie to you."

Jason said, "I'll go first."

The top of the stepladder reached just short of the
trap door. Jason could stand on the next-to-last rung
and push the hole's cover aside. "It's a big attic," he
told them. "I think we can climb in all right. There's
some light from those little shuttered places under
the gables. There's a lot of junk up here. Old furniture and boxes and things."

"I bet they're my great-great-great-grandmother's
things!" Gale said breathlessly. "I bet we do find
something—something about the secret of the seven
crows, after all!"

They crowded after Jason into the attic, helping
Bug and Patricia up, then looking around curiously.
It would take a lot of exploring to examine all that
junk, Shelley thought. But it would be fun.

"What's that?" They all froze as a rustle in a
dusky corner turned into a swoop of wings.

"It's bats!" Pam screamed. "Let me out of here!"
She held her arms over her head protectively. "If they
get in your hair you'll go crazy—"

"Chase 'em out, Dracula!" Bug said. Dracula stayed on Gale's shoulder. "He's got too much sense to tangle with bats," Bug said.

As suddenly as they had swooped, the bats were quiet again. "Maybe they went out the window," Shelley hoped. "They do make the place smell awful."

"I don't think they're dangerous," Jason said soothingly to Pam. "They just hang on the rafters and sleep—if you leave them alone."

"I'll leave them alone all right," Pam said fervently.

"There's the machine Cap'n Boney brought up here," Michael told them, pointing. "And the boxes next to it."

"Wonder what he made with that thing?" Jason said, poking at it, puzzled. "Why would he be hiding stuff like that up here? It doesn't look like any treasure. The boxes aren't old."

"Maybe he made counterfeit money," Pam said. "I heard about somebody who did that. It was in his basement, though. And he was caught."

"I don't see how it could be that," Jason said. "You have to have something more like a printing press for counterfeit money."

"There's more stuff in these big boxes," Patricia said helpfully. "Look—it's white powder—"

Shelley reached over to help her open another, and Jason tugged at the top of the box. It came loose suddenly, and spilled out some tiny metal boxes like the ones Dracula had found in the priest's house. "What in the world? They look like aspirin boxes, only smaller."

"And look—here are pills in this other big box. Millions of pills!" Pam said.

"I bet this is a pill-making machine," Jason said. "I read about what pushers do when they're pushing speed. That's what they call amphetamines. They can get the powder form of it in Mexico cheap, and smuggle it into this country and make it into pills and sell 'em to school kids—or anybody—for a quarter apiece. It would be easy for somebody who had a good way to go to Mexico secretly—like a shrimp boat—"

"That explains why Cap'n Boney didn't bother much about bringing back shrimp," Gale said thoughtfully, "and this is the stuff that guy Dolph is after. Not the treasure. Maybe Cap'n Boney brought in the stuff and made the pills and Dolph was the one who sold them. Patricia heard they were in business together, remember."

They were all concentrating on the boxes and their contents, and off guard. Then Shelley glanced up and saw something move, at the edge of the trap door.

It was a hand. A large sun-tanned hand, a man's grimy big old hand, catching hold of the edge. Then another hand gripped the other side of the hole, and somebody's shaggy black hair showed in the opening.

Somebody had followed them. They must have forgotten to lock the door behind them.

Somebody was there on the ladder—cutting off the only way to get out of the attic.

Shelley screamed.

The Six Crows Are Found

"It's him!" Gale cried as the man's face appeared. "It's him all right!"

"Just get out of my way, kids," Dolph said, his voice low and threatening. As he stood on the ladder his head and shoulders blocked the opening. "I don't want to have to hurt you. Just don't bother me. Stand over there by the wall while I—"

"What do you want?" Jason said. Shelley thought he looked very brave. His voice cracked as he said it, but he couldn't help that.

"Yes, what is it you want?" she asked, trying to back Jason up. Her own voice trembled and her insides felt shaky. She knew Jason must be quivery inside, too. But you couldn't tell it to look at him.

"All I want is what's mine, little lady," Dolph said. Shelley hated being called little lady. She could have snatched his eyeballs out, just for that. She wished

she'd had on her hard shoes—maybe she'd have had enough courage to stomp on his hands or kick him in the face as he stood in the opening. But with sneakers —well, she probably wouldn't have dared do it any- how.

Dolph went on, "Just the stuff in them boxes, that's all. I paid for it and I'm not about to lose my money because Boney Willis got hisself killed— Now you move out of my way, boy, if you don't want to get killed just as dead as Boney."

Jason said, shakily, "We know what it is and—"

"Don't, Jason!" Gale cried a warning. "Don't say—" But it was too late to stop Jason from rashly exposing his dangerous guess.

"We know you're a drug pusher and you're going to catch it when Dad—"

"And I know your Dad won't be back for a couple of hours," Dolph said unpleasantly. "I'll be long gone."

"He read the note too," Pam whispered. "He fol- lowed us up here after he couldn't find the stuff in the priest's house. Uncle Jonathan said to keep the doors locked, and we forgot."

"So get out of my way, all of you, before I knock you out," Dolph finished, moving a step higher up into the attic.

There was a swoop of wings again—Shelley felt the rush past her head—but this time it was Dracula, dive-bombing the man. Dolph yelled an obscene word as he dodged the surprise attack and struck out at Dracula, almost losing his balance. Bug cried, "Good old Dracula!" as the bird flew in for a second pecking at the man's eyes. And Bug flung himself into the fray to help Dracula.

Jason said, "Everybody—get him! Don't let him get in!"

There was heroic confusion as Shelley and Pam and Gale and Michael and Patricia all launched themselves after Jason and Bug toward the man in the trap door. Their rush made him stumble backward, and he disappeared from view.

Then another man's voice said, "What's goin' on here?" and the kids above, crowding around the opening, saw that Dolph had fallen almost on top of a large black man who had an iron grip on him. "What are you doin' to my kids?"

"Pop!" Michael and Patricia shrieked.

"Roscoe!" Gale yelled. "Roscoe to the rescue! Hold him, Roscoe! He's a drug pusher!"

Roscoe Lummus was twisting the snarling, cursing man's arms behind him, and Shelley let out her breath she had been holding. Clearly Roscoe was much stronger than Dolph.

"And what are you doin' here?" Roscoe said severely to Michael and Patricia. "Your ma told me she thought you'd gone off with Gale and some of her friends, and she had told you to stay in the yard. So I came after you. What're you doin' up there anyhow? Come down."

"Nothin'," Michael answered. They all climbed down the ladder.

"Aw, Pop—" Patricia said.

"They were just helping us, Mr. Lummus," Shelley said.

"He said he was going to kill Jason," Pam said, and now that the danger was over, she sounded as if she might be going to cry.

Shelley said, "He didn't really mean *kill*. Don't worry, Pam."

Gale said, "Hey, Roscoe, did you know Cap'n Boney was bringing in speed and that kind of stuff from Mexico?"

"I didn't know what he was bringin'," Roscoe said. "He told me to mind my own business and I could have all the fish and shrimp. So I did. You don't reckon I'll get in trouble for that, do you, Gale? I never even saw the stuff, much less make anything out of it. I just ran the boat and handled the nets."

"No, 'course you won't get in trouble," Jason assured him. "You caught this guy and maybe saved our lives! You ought to get a reward—I'm going to run down and bring some rope I've got in my room and we'll tie him up. Then when Dad comes—"

"There he is now!" Bug said. "I hear the car." He ran down the stairs, calling, "Dad! Come quick!" and Jason followed.

They came back with Daddy and Mama and the rope, talking both together, trying to explain what had happened. "He's a pusher, Dad! He was trying to get the stuff that Cap'n Boney hid in our attic."

"You can't prove nothin'," Dolph said sullenly. "You can't prove I'm a pusher."

"You said that stuff is yours!" Jason answered. "You said you paid for it and you came to get it. We all heard you. All the police have to do is test it and see if it's speed or something worse!"

Dad was tying the man's hands as Roscoe held him, and then his feet, after which Roscoe pushed Dolph contemptuously down on the floor. "That'll hold you for a while," he said with satisfaction. "Try to hurt my kids, will you?" and he caught Patricia up in his arms and hugged her. Shelley looked at Daddy hopefully, but he didn't seem to think of doing that to her. He was too busy saying, "Now, Jason, what happened?" And Jason told him.

"Yes, I think with the things in the attic for evidence, and your testimony that he claimed them for his, the authorities will have a pretty good case against this man," Daddy said. "I'll go and call them. Thank you, Mr. Lummus, for helping the kids out of a dangerous spot. I believe you'll be in the clear when it's all explained. Capturing this one will certainly be in your favor."

"Thank you, Mr. Calhoun," Roscoe said. "Now I'll take Michael and Patricia home to their ma. She'll be wonderin' what happened to them. And they're goin' to catch it for not stayin' in the yard when they were told!"

"Aw, don't punish them, Roscoe," Gale said. "They were a big help. We couldn't have found the stuff if they hadn't told us where to look."

"I knew where it was," Michael said. "I'd have told, as soon as I thought about what it might be."

"Well, don't punish them anyhow, huh?" Gale coaxed. "They're pretty good kids."

Daddy said, "I'll put in a good word for them, too, Mr. Lummus," and Shelley knew that meant he wasn't going to tell on Michael and Patricia for being poltergeists.

"Well—" Roscoe said, "maybe it won't be too much of a lickin'. I'll tell their ma to just use a little bitty peach tree switch." He grinned, and Michael and Patricia grinned too, and went off each one swinging to one of Roscoe's hands.

"Pay you tomorrow," Jason called after them.

"Never mind," Michael called back. "You don't have to. I reckon we ought to've told anyhow. Let it go to pay for the broken china and stuff."

"Well, O.K.," Jason said, because that would make their consciences clear.

Then they had to tell Daddy and Mama how all the tricks were pulled.

The police came at last, heard the story, and took Dolph and the boxes and the pill-making machine away. Everything was suddenly in the quiet of anti-climax. Mama said, "By the way, Jason, I don't suppose you had time, in between finding amphetamines in the attic and apprehending criminals, to start anything for supper?"

"I forgot all about supper!" Jason groaned. "I'm sorry, Mama. I meant to. But I guess there really wasn't time. And I'm hungry, too! I wish I did have something good ready."

"Can't we—" Pam and Shelley and Bug said all together, "go to the drive-in and have hamburgers and french fries for supper tonight?"

"That sounds like the only thing to do," Mama said, smiling. "Gale, won't you come too? We can wait while you ask your father."

"And Dracula can come too," Bug said. "Did you see how me and Dracula dived at that guy? Pow, right in the eyes! I've got to train me a crow."

"I'd like to, Mrs. Calhoun," Gale said, and Shelley could tell she really wanted like everything to go to the drive-in with them. "But I guess I'd better not. My father depends on me to take care of him and fix his supper and all."

"We could bring him a hamburger and french fries," Pam said, but Gale still said she couldn't.

"He doesn't like hamburgers. Thanks just the same."

"Come back after supper, then," Pam said. "It's important. I've got something to tell you all." She looked mysterious, and wouldn't tell any of them what it was. Her voice sounded tense with suppressed excitement.

When they got back from the drive-in, Jason told Mama, "Tomorrow night I'll fix one of my special gourmet dinners, Mama! I meant to, tonight, if we hadn't got involved in the attic. And I'll make the Key lime pie, too."

"Can I count on that?" Mama said, but she smiled. "It's all right, Jason."

"Sometimes hamburgers are good, for a change from all that gourmet stuff of Jason's," Bug said innocently, and ducked.

Jason said, "Just for that, Bug, you can wait till

tomorrow to see what Pam found in the attic. She's going to show it to us, right now!" He had seen Gale and Dracula coming.

"What?" Shelley urged Pam, in new excitement. "Tell us quick!"

Pam said, "I want to let Bug in on it too, Jason. He didn't mean anything."

"Well, O.K." Jason hadn't really meant to leave Bug out; he just wanted to subdue him a little. "You and Mama want to come too?" he asked Dad.

"The excitement has worn us out," Dad said from his easy chair opposite Mama's, in the living room. "Why don't you just bring it down and show us later?"

"O.K.," Jason said. "Bug, get the flashlight." Shelley thought he seemed to be trying to take over from Pam, and Pam was letting him.

"What is it?" Gale could hardly wait. "When did you find it?" she asked Pam.

"I saw it while we were getting into those boxes of pills and all," Pam said. "But things started happening so fast, I thought I'd better not say anything right then. Nobody had noticed it but me, so I knew it'd be perfectly safe." She took the flashlight from Bug.

"What would?" Shelley quivered with suspense.

Pam stopped at the foot of the ladder to the attic, with the flashlight in her hand, because the attic didn't have electric lights. "Up there," she said solemnly, "on the floor, behind one of the old trunks on the other side from the pill-making machine—I saw the six crows!"

The Indecipherable Cipher

"You saw them? Six of them?" Shelley could hardly believe there were six stuffed crows—or any kind of crows—up there that she had missed seeing. "And were they in a box?"

The others crowded into the attic behind Pam, a bit fearfully, because of the bats, not ghosts. Dracula muttered his usual caw-imprecations, and Bug was sure he was telling the bats to stay away. "They aren't exactly in a box. But they're boxed, like she said."

To Shelley the whole place smelled so horribly like bats, she wished there were windows they could open. But Pam's find made her forget to try not to breathe the smell.

Pam picked up a box from behind a hump-backed trunk.

"Wow!" Bug said.

Jason said, "Let me see," and Pam gave it to him.

It was a small, once-gilded box, about six by eight inches, that might have held a lady's jewelry or gloves or handkerchiefs. The gilt was tarnished, and the top had a set-in picture under glass.

"A *picture* of six crows!" Shelley cried out. You could count them at a glance, sitting on a tree branch.

"A pen-and-ink sketch," Jason corrected her happily, again taking over. "Maybe Mrs. Crawley drew them herself. The box probably had a different top when she bought it. But she fixed it up—because of the clues. She had to have six crows to reveal a clue."

"And the box was gold then," Shelley said doubtfully. "Could that be all the gold she meant in 'six crows for gold'?"

"What's in it?" Pam said practically. "Maybe there's the gold?"

Jason handed the box to Gale, and she lifted the lid.

The box was empty. The hinged lid had a mirror for the inside instead of a lining.

"Well, if there was gold here, somebody else got it. Probably Cap'n Boney," Shelley said disappointedly.

"Maybe we should look in the trunk it was behind," Gale said. "Or in some of the other things up here."

"We'll have to look in all of them, I guess," Jason said, "if we don't find the seven crows first. If this is the six crows—and the gold—then we're on the last lap. The 'secret that's never been told.' We'll have to wait till tomorrow, though, to examine the trunks and all. The flashlight battery's getting weak."

Gale wanted to keep on looking but Shelley said, "Let's go show the box to Mama and Daddy." She needed some air to breathe that didn't smell like bats —that awful ratty smell.

Down in the living room again, they all crowded around while Daddy looked over the box. "So somebody already cleaned out the gold? If it held gold?" he said. "Maybe Cap'n Boney noticed it when he put in the stuff he hid up here, and took the gold without the box?"

"But he'd never have thought the box meant anything," Jason pointed out. "He didn't know anything about the clues—the six crows wouldn't have meant gold to him."

Gale was so disappointed she could hardly speak. Shelley could see that she thought the secret was lost to them.

"Well, we still have the seventh clue—the seven crows," she said, putting her arm around Gale and giving her a hug. "Maybe the secret that's never been told will have something to do with the gold."

"That secret's got to be something awful," Gale said pessimistically. "If it had been anything good about the Crawleys, they would have told it."

"Wait a minute!" Shelley said. "I've just thought of something. The note from the chapel! It said 'seven crows behind six crows.' Daddy, will that glass come off the top of the box?"

"We'll see," Daddy said, his interest quickening. "Go and get my small screwdriver, Bug."

"That's good thinking, Shelley!" Jason said, and she thought she detected an unaccustomed respect in his voice. Warmth swelled in her heart.

Carefully Daddy pried the frame off. The glass and the mirror came apart. Between them and behind the pen-and-ink sketch—"Behind the six crows, all right!" Shelley exclaimed—were two sheets of thin paper.

Daddy looked at her then, a rather special look. "It *was* good thinking, Shelley." The warmth in her breast expanded until she thought it might burst like a balloon. It was Shelley he was praising, not Jason!

"It was Pam who found the box," she pointed out modestly.

"Just luck," Pam said, but Shelley knew she was pleased when Jason cuffed her with a soft fist and Daddy said, "Good for Pam, too."

"Look here—" Gale had taken up the thin sheets of paper.

On one, the words "Seven Crows" were written in faded ink. "Here's the seven crows—but they're just the words, not pictures and not real crows either!" she said.

A tiny gold key, about half an inch long, was glued down on the paper, under the writing.

"Wow!" Bug said again. "Here's the gold! If we only knew what it opens!"

"We'd better find what it opens, before Dracula steals it," Pam said. "It's not a key to the box, because that doesn't have any lock at all."

On the other thin sheet of paper were two lines of strange letters and figures that didn't make any sense:

$$s_5 e_4 e_2 n_1 o_2 v_1 o_2 n_2 v_3 w_2 v_1 e_3 s_1 v_3 w_1 w_2 e_1 s_5 o_2 w_1 n_1$$
$$e_2 v_3 o_1 s_1 s_4 n_3 n_2 s_5 w_2 n_1 n_1 s_3$$

Shelley said, dismayed, "The secret that's never been told is in code!"

Daddy said, "I'm no code expert, but it looks like a hard one to decipher."

"We'll ask Mr. Dilmous!" Gale said. "Maybe he's a code expert."

"He hasn't done too well so far," Shelley said skeptically. "He hasn't even figured out what the note hidden in the bedpost meant. And it's in plain English."

"At least," Jason said thoughtfully, "we can still hope there's a box somewhere with the treasure in it. Because the gold key has to open *some*thing, and since it's gold—"

Gale cheered up a little at that. "Right," she said. "We'll keep looking in the attic for some box it'll open. We might just luck into it, while Mr. Dilmous is trying to figure out the code."

"Tomorrow will be a busy day," Pam said.

"Looks like I won't get much more work out of you kids till you finish that treasure hunt," Daddy said good-naturedly. "So hurry up and find the gold or the secret or whatever it is. We've got a job on our hands, to finish the school building before fall."

"We're trying!" Shelley said earnestly. "And when we do—you can buy Crauleia! See, Daddy, that's why we're trying so hard. Mr. Franklin would sell it to you if he knew the treasure had been found and there wasn't any reason to keep Crauleia in their family any more. And Gale would be the legal heir so he could sell it for her."

"I know," Daddy said, but Shelley could tell he wasn't exactly optimistic. "That's why I'm letting you all off work tomorrow." He went back to his newspaper.

Shelley walked with Gale and Dracula out to the road. "You see," Gale said, "your father did give you credit for thinking of looking behind the six crows."

"I don't know," Shelley said. "If it had been Jason, he'd've set off fireworks!"

"You're hopeless," Gale said, but Shelley thought she didn't mean it. "Goodnight."

" 'Night." Dracula said something and Shelley added, "You, too, Dracula."

The next morning early, as soon after breakfast as Gale and Dracula arrived, they took the code message to Mr. Dilmous. Jason had copied it off carefully; he wanted to keep the original in the box, to puzzle over for himself. "Maybe I'll be a code expert myself, Shell," he told her. "I've read a little about it."

Mr. Dilmous shook his head when he saw the coded message. He reached up on a shelf and took down a thick dark green book. Shelley noted its title: *Handy Book of Literary Curiosities,* by Walsh. "I think it's in here," Mr. Dilmous said.

"You mean, you recognize it, sir?" Jason said in high excitement. "You mean you've got a book that tells how to break this code?"

"I wish I did," Mr. Dilmous said, smiling. "No, all I have is a book that tells what the code is—not how to decipher it. You see, it apparently is a good example of something I recognized from reading about it not long ago—a code that its French originators called the *chiffre indéchiffrable*, meaning 'the indecipherable cipher.' "

"You mean—we can't ever read it?" Shelley asked. "But, Mr. Dilmous, we're sure that's the secret! The secret that's never been told!"

"How does it work?" Jason said. "What makes it indecipherable?"

Mr. Dilmous read from the book, "It was an extension of the principle of substituting one letter of the alphabet for another. A new element was introduced—a key word that was known only to the sender and the receiver. When the lattter received the message, he wrote the key word over the letters . . ."

Jason said, "I think I see. We used to make up a code by letting *a* be *b* and *b* be *c* and so on. This is much harder. How did Mrs. Crawley expect any of her descendants to find the right word, though? She sure must have thought you'd be a brain, Gale!"

"Well, I'm not," Gale said dejectedly. "I couldn't even get the first clue till you kids came to help me. I didn't even have enough sense to look at the woodwork in the chapel or to hunt in the attic—that seemed too hard to do by myself— Oh, I forgot to tell you. About the 'five crows for silver.' My father heard from the coin dealer in New Jersey. He said there were seven hundred of these silver dollars minted. It was called 'the San Francisco silver dollar' because it was minted in San Francisco; that's why it has S on it. Well, not one of those seven hundred has ever been reported in anybody's collection. That makes it so rare that it might be real valuable. The dealer didn't actually make my father an offer for it, but he said if it was authenticated and offered on the market, it could break all the records for a U.S. coin. A man who owns one of the 1913 Liberty nickels has turned down $100,000 for his nickel. And there are five of those known. So—"

"That's great!" Pam said. "Aren't you glad, Gale? You'll be rich. You don't even need to find the gold."

Gale was pessimistic, as usual. "I bet it can't be the right one. I bet there are plenty of 1873 S silver dollars somewhere. Why should my great-great-great-grand-mother have the only one?"

"Well, you might not get $100,000 for it, but I'm sure it has considerable value," Mr. Dilmous said. "It's amazing how much a collector will pay for some-thing he wants, if he has plenty of money."

"But find a collector who wants it!" Gale said. "Be-sides, it's not in good condition. It's got a hole in it."

"If it were mine, I'd keep it—not sell it at all," Shelley said. "Think of that young girl all that long time ago, fixing up that dollar on a ribbon for her baby to cut his teeth on. I don't see how you can bear for your Dad to sell it, Gale! It's like selling part of your family."

Gale said, "I'm not sentimental like you, Shelley. I guess I couldn't bear for him *not* to sell it, we need the money so bad. You've no idea. See, he hasn't been able to work for a while, and we didn't have anything worth selling but Crauleia, and we can't sell it till we find the secret. So I'd guess my great-great-great-grandmother would be glad for her last descendant to sell the dollar and have a little money to pay for groceries."

"Well, if you put it that way—" Shelley agreed, but regretfully. Gale was right; she was sentimental. Was that a bad thing to be? Realists got along better, Jason had once told her. But Shelley thought maybe she'd rather have that soft, melancholy feeling inside her than to be hard-boiled and practical about everything.

Mr. Dilmous said, "I haven't exactly decoded your note from the bedpost yet, but I did find the quotations in *Julius Caesar*. The one about 'Remember March—the Ides of March remember' is from Act IV, Scene 3; Brutus is speaking. And 'Night hangs upon mine eyes; my bones would rest' is in Act V, Scene 5, also Brutus. The passage about 'All the conspirators save only he—' is from Act V, Scene 5, too—said about Brutus by Antony. If you remember the Shakespeare play, Brutus killed Caesar. So this old man who wrote the note was apparently somehow identifying himself with Brutus. But I don't find any acrostic, or any way he revealed anything else about himself."

164|

"Some crazy people think they're Napoleon," Gale said. "He thought he was that guy Brutus."

"Well, it's interesting, but unless we can find the gold he said he was leaving to Mrs. Crawley, it's not much good to us," Jason said. "Thanks, Mr. Dilmous. Please keep thinking of some way to break that code message, though. I read something about how they break codes by figuring out how many times a certain symbol is used, and the one used oftenest is probably e, and I think it said i is the next oftenest used, and so on. I plan to keep working on it myself."

"I'm afraid we won't be able to break it that way," Mr. Dilmous said dubiously. "Notice how this one uses certain letters over and over, with small different numbers attached to them. I'm sure that has some significance, but I'm at a loss to think what significance. Mrs. Howard Townsend Crawley must have been a remarkable woman."

"She sure did like to hide things," Gale grumbled. "She might have been part crow herself."

"Maybe she turned into a crow at midnight on the night of the full moon," Jason said. "Like werewolves. Were there any were-crows, Mr. Dilmous?"

"I never heard of any," Mr. Dilmous said. "But it's a fascinating idea. You work on it, Jason."

"I may have time to research it sometime, sir," Jason said. "But not today. Dad let us off working on the house to try to find the treasure. We're going to look

through Mrs. Crawley's old stuff in the attic. If we're lucky, we might find something relevant, even if we can't decipher the code." [|]

"Keep me informed," said Mr. Dilmous. "You might, at that."

"Would you like one of Otto's puppies, sir?" Bug said. "I don't think Mama's going to let us keep them all. They'll make swell watchdogs. Of course, they're too young yet to give away, but when they're weaned—"

"They're real cute," Pam said. "I'm going to take one home with me."

"I'd love to see them," Mr. Dilmous said, but he didn't promise to take one.

As they straggled home, Shelley reminded Jason, "Don't forget, you promised Mama to cook dinner tonight. Let's not get so interested in the attic that we'll forget that again! We'll help you, though."

"Thanks, Shell. Maybe you can do a few things, like grate the lime rind for the pie. But like I said, I'm training Bug. He'll make a good chef someday."

"What're we having?" Pam asked.

"I thought maybe *coq au vin*," Jason said. "I noticed Mama bought chicken. And there's some wine left from that time I made *bœuf bourguignon*. But I'm afraid fowl calls for white wine, and that was red. Burgundy. I'll have to look it up."

He checked the supplies when they got home, and found everything he needed. "I'm in luck—this recipe uses Burgundy too," he told Shelley. "There's plenty left. I can start about 4:30 and everything will be ready to eat by seven or 7:30," he calculated. "So we have a good long time to check out the stuff in the attic. With a short break for lunch."

"Why don't we have lunch first?" Bug said. "I'm hungry."

"Good idea," Gale said. "I ought to go and see about my father's. So you all eat while I'm gone. Wait for me before you tackle the attic, though!"

"We will," Shelley promised.

But although the smelly attic had a lot of great stuff in it—like feather fans, and moth-eaten old-fashioned clothes, and even some toys that Jason said would bring a lot of money as antiques, and fascinating odds and ends they couldn't even guess the purpose of—there was no trace of the gold, nor any box the little gold key might open, nor any clue to the code word.

"I hoped we'd find her diary or something like that," Gale said, "and that she'd put the word in it. But she must not have kept any diary. I wish she'd left me a note of some kind, to tell me how to decipher that stuff!"

"You're supposed to be smart enough to figure it out by yourself," Pam said.

Shelley said, "I wish the old bats didn't smell up the place so. I'm going downstairs—I can't stand it any longer."

"We've looked at everything, anyhow," Pam said.

"And it's time to start dinner," Jason said. "I've got to shower, though, before I can cook. So has anybody who's going to help," he added sternly. "This is a dirty old place."

"Come on, Gale, you can use our bathroom," Shelley said. "The boys use the one at the other end of the hall."

"Dracula can come with us," Bug said. "He's a boy."

"Thanks, but we'll go on home," Gale said. "If anything happens, let me know."

"I'll save you a piece of my pie," Jason said kindly. "It's probably the best pie in the world."

Dracula said something that sounded like, "Aw—now!"

"It really is, Dracula," Bug said earnestly. "He'll save you a piece, too."

"You save that bird a piece of *yours*," Jason recommended as Gale and Dracula left, "if you want him to have any."

When everybody had cleaned up (and he inspected Bug's fingernails), Jason put Shelley to work grating lime rinds and Bug to setting out the utensils he would need. "Pam, you can look at the recipes and get out all the supplies I'm going to use, and put them on the table. Put the pie stuff here and the chicken stuff over there."

"What are *you* going to be doing all this time?" Pam asked with sarcasm, but she obediently began to bring out the flour and sugar and butter.

"Concentrating," Jason said grandly. "Cooking a gourmet meal requires concentration, you know. I really ought to be alone."

"That'll be easy to arrange," Bug said impudently. "We'll all split, won't we, girls?"

"Never mind," Jason said. "Do your job and don't talk so much! Grandma, get your tail out of the cream pitcher! Bug, keep her off the table. That's another job for you."

He put the cut-up chicken in a skillet with melted butter, to brown slowly, and started on the pie.

Shelley brought him the grated rind. The pungent lime scent tickled her nostrils. "It smells lovely," she said. "Like a cool breeze on a hot day. Key lime pie is the best stuff!"

"Why is it called Key lime pie?" Bug asked.

"I don't know," Jason told him, "unless it was invented on the Florida Keys, and the limes that grow down there are called Key limes, and—wait a minute! Key! That's it! The key to the code! She was telling us—and all the time we never guessed! Not even Mr. Dilmous guessed!"

"What are you talking about?" Shelley gasped; he seemed to be saying he knew how to decipher the code message. But he wasn't really making sense. "What do you—?"

"I think I know how to read the code," Jason said in high excitement. "I think I can decipher the indecipherable cipher! At least, I know the key word!"

Under the Crow's Claw

"What is it, then?" Shelley and Pam said together. It couldn't be limes.

"I can't stop to decipher it now," Jason said, grinning fiendishly, "so I might as well keep you all in suspense a while longer. I'll give you a clue, though—it was in the box."

They puzzled over that all through dinner, which Jason grandly announced was "a triumph of culinary art." Even Daddy and Mama couldn't guess what the key word was, but they agreed that the food was as elegant as Jason claimed.

While Shelley and Pam hurriedly cleaned up the kitchen, Bug went to rush Gale and Dracula, and Jason sat down to try to decipher the strange message. Even though he was certain of the key word now, it wasn't easy to decide exactly how to use it. But he was determined not to turn this one over to Mr. Dilmous.

The others crowded around him as he sat at the table with paper and pencil and the note from under the box's top. "Back off!" he said. "Give me room. I think I'm getting it now. Yes, this must be right. There are six *e*'s and five *s*'s and three *c*'s and —yes, this is working out all right.

"See," he explained, his voice changing from low to high and back several times with excitement, "the key word is 'seven crows.' That's what Mrs. Crawley meant by putting the words 'seven crows' on the piece of paper with the gold key. She was telling us, 'The key is seven crows.' Not real crows, like we thought at first, just the letters in the words. Now if we do what Mr. Dilmous said, and write the letters in those two words above the letters of the alphabet, like this:

s e v e n c r o w s s e v e n c r o w s s e v e n c
a b c d e f g h i j k l m n o p q r s t u v w x y z

we have too many of the same letter for the message to make sense. But if we mark each time the letter is used, with a number, we get an alphabet with each letter having a different symbol. *A* is *s*-1, *b* is *e*-1, *c* is *v*-1, *d* is *e*-2, *e* is *n*-1, and so on. Like this:

s_1 e_1 v_1 e_2 n_1 c_1 r_1 o_1 w_1 s_2 s_3 e_3 v_2 e_4 n_2 c_2 r_2
a   b   c   d   e   f   g   h   i   j   k   l   m   n   o   p   q

o_2 w_2 s_4 s_5 e_5 v_3 e_6 n_3 c_3
r   s   t   u   v   w   x   y   z

Then the message goes like this:

s_5 e_4 e_2 n_1 o_2 v_1 o_2 n_2 v_3 w_2 v_1 e_3 s_1 v_3 w_1 w_2

u n d e r c r o w s c l a w i s

e_1 s_5 o_2 w_1 n_1 e_2 v_3 o_1 s_1 s_4 n_3 n_2 s_5 w_2 n_1 n_1 s_3

b u r i e d w h a t y o u s e e k

Shelley read off as Jason wrote it down, " 'Under crow's claw is buried what you seek.' "

Gale said fiercely, "I give up! She's supposed to tell us the secret when we find the seven crows! Now we found it—or rather, Jason did—and she tells us to find something else! It's not fair. I hate my great-great-great-grandmother. I'm not going to play her game any more. She's—somewhere—just laughing at us for thinking we had the secret worked out."

"I know how you feel," Shelley said sympathetically. "But look at it as a challenge, Gale! Don't let her make you quit. She really wanted you to find it, you said once. You even thought her ghost was trying to help you in the search. So maybe she'll help us find the crow's claw."

"Let's look at this thing logically," Jason said. "Since she says it's buried, more than likely it's outdoors. We've been looking inside the house. The will said, 'the house and all that's in it and around it.' There has to be a reason for saying 'around it' too. She must have buried the gold somewhere around the outside of the house. So we have to look for a crow's claw outside the house. Maybe she carved one on a rock or a tree. Maybe she made the shape of a claw out of rocks, and buried the stuff under them. Tomorrow morning we'll search every inch of ground around here for anything that looks like a crow's claw. Come early, Gale."

"O.K.," Gale agreed, cheering up a little at Shelley's and Jason's pep talk.

Shelley could hardly sleep, all night. Anticipation made her senses keenly aware; she heard katydids and night birds and Pam's even breathing and the screak of the springs when she turned over. She smelled the salt air blowing in the window; she saw in her mind's eye the shape of a crow's claw outlined in rocks on white sand. (But, she thought, over all these years somebody might have moved them. Unless they're great big rocks. And in that case we'd have to be in an airplane to see the shape of the claw. We probably won't even recognize it when we see it.) She felt the texture of the smooth sheet as her finger drew a claw shape on it. Restlessly she turned and punched her pillow and at last fell asleep.

After breakfast Jason wanted to postpone the hunt for the crow's claw until they could show Mr. Dilmous how the code had worked out. Shelley was eager to get started on the search. But Jason won, as usual. She suspected he only wanted to show Mr. Dilmous how clever he was. He had already demonstrated to Daddy and Mama how he had figured out the code, and had been praised by them, naturally.

Mr. Dilmous was delighted with Jason too. "Maybe you ought to be a cryptographer for the C.I.A., some day," he said. "It would be an interesting career."

"Maybe I will, unless I decide to be a master chef," Jason said. "I think master chefs might make more money. The government doesn't pay too well, I've heard."

"Let's go look for the crow's claw," Bug said. He had Dracula on his shoulder, murmuring into his ear as if the crow were prompting him.

"Yes," Shelley said. "We're wasting time."

"Why don't you come with us, Mr. Dilmous?" Gale said. "You might be able to see it when we couldn't."

"And you could see Otto's puppies," Bug said, "and pick out the one you want."

Mr. Dilmous said he'd go with them to look for the crow's claw, but he really didn't think he could accept a puppy.

"Why is it people don't want puppies?" Bug said mournfully to Dracula. "Mama doesn't want them— and Mr. Dilmous doesn't want even one—and I think it'd be just great to have a hundred puppies! Don't you, Dracula?" The crow cawed softly and nodded, as if he agreed. "But what would a crow do with a hundred puppies?"

When they got back home, Daddy was outside trying to figure out the best way to remove the old uprooted cedar that was leaning perilously against the house. Jason introduced Mr. Dilmous, who recommended a man he knew who had cut out some of the trees around Gulf Springs that the hurricane had left damaged beyond saving. Daddy said he'd try first, himself, to get it out by sawing it in parts with a chain-saw he'd rented. If he couldn't, though, he'd be glad to get the man Mr. Dilmous suggested.

All this time, Shelley and the rest were impatiently waiting. "Come on, Mr. Dilmous!" Bug urged. "You can talk to Dad all day after you help us find the crow's claw."

They systematically examined every rock and tree around the house, but after two hours of sand in their sneakers and cockspurs on their clothes, they were tired of looking. Showing signs of exhaustion, Mr. Dilmous said he believed he'd go and look at the puppies now. Pam went with him. She had already picked out her puppy, and one each for her sisters if her mother would let Pam and Margaret and Elizabeth each have one for her own, which Pam realized wasn't the least bit likely.

The others sat down on the kitchen doorstep to rest. "I told you my great-great-great-grandmother was crazy," Gale grumbled. "There probably isn't any crow's claw or any treasure either. She was just putting us on, I'll bet."

"Dad's cutting on that cedar, and we haven't looked at it," Jason said. "The crow's claw might be carved on it."

"It's the only one we haven't looked at, then," Shelley said.

"Hey, Dad!" Jason said. "Let us look at this tree before you do something to it. Have you seen any carving on it?"

"Not a bit," Daddy said, but he stopped and helped

them look. The gray bark was weatherworn and felt silver to the touch, Shelley thought. The tree hung onto life, although only a few of its roots were left in the ground; sparse green had sprouted on limbs that looked dead, and the lacy sprigs smelled cedary when you broke them off. Most of the roots were out of the ground; a huge hole, partly washed in with sand now, showed how deeply it had grown in the ground.

"Look," Bug said. "Dracula's got him a girl friend." Dracula and another crow were perched together on the tree's roots.

"I don't know how you'd know it's a girl," Pam said.

Gale said strangely, " 'Two crows for joy—' *We're going to find it here.*"

Shelley gasped, "Look at the root they're on! Doesn't it—with those other big roots right there— don't they look just like Dracula's claw? The part that was out of the ground at the foot of the tree— and made a sort of curved hollow—"

"They do! They do!" Jason shouted. "That *could* be the crow's claw! Wow, Shelley! that's great seeing."

"Dracula found it," Bug said. "Good old Dracula! He found it for Gale!"

Mr. Dilmous and Pam came out of the priest's house when Jason shouted, and hurried over to the tree. Mr. Dilmous and Daddy and Jason calculated about where those particular roots had been when the tree was upright in the sandy earth, and Jason ran for a shovel and started to dig.

With the sound of the shovel cutting through sand, and the sand falling as he threw it out of the hole, Shelley thought she couldn't stand it. Her throat was tight with excitement.

Jason said, "I think I've found something." His voice went high and then choked down with eagerness.

"Careful," Mr. Dilmous warned. "It might be decayed and crumbly—whatever it is."

Jason was down in the hole now, scrabbling in the sand with his hands. "It's here!" he said. Then he saw Gale. "Come on down, Gale. You've got to be the one to find the secret of the seven crows—so Crauleia can be yours."

Gale scrambled down in the hole with him. The others crowded the edge to see what was there. Bug got too close, and the edge caved in, tumbling him on top of Gale and Jason. Dracula flew off to a nearby pine tree, to discuss it with the other crow. Shelley thought, Two crows for joy. How strange that it really was like the verse. Joy for Gale. A coincidence, of course, but still . . .

Out of the confusion, Gale emerged, standing up and holding up a little rusted metal box in both hands. It wasn't decayed at all. It was small enough to go inside the other box topped with the six crows. And this one had a tiny padlock.

"I guess here's where the little gold key fits," Jason said, climbing out of the hole with a hand up from Daddy, and reaching back for Gale. "Bug"— he pulled

him out last—"run get the key. It's on the desk in our room."

"She might have kept this box inside that other box, before she decided to bury it," Gale speculated. "It would go in it, all right."

The little gold key did fit the small padlock. It opened with a click, and Gale lifted the lid of the rusty box. Everybody gasped.

This time there was gold. In the box lay about a double handful of tarnished gold coins, of different sizes, stamped with eagles and Indians' heads. A folded paper, again with that faded handwriting, lay under them.

"Read it," Jason urged Gale. "I hope she didn't use a code this time—"

She hadn't. Gale unfolded the note slowly and read aloud, " 'This is the money Mr. Marcus, the old man who said he was John Wilkes Booth, wanted me to have—' "

"John Wilkes Booth!" Mr. Dilmous said. "Of course! I should have known who J. W. B. had to be. The reference to tyrants, and the words of Marcus Brutus, and all that— But it's not true, of course. He couldn't have been John Wilkes Booth. Booth was killed trying to get away after he shot Lincoln."

Gale read on, " 'He could not spend it because it was "blood money," he said, and neither can I, for the same reason. I do not know whether he was really Booth or not, but I am convinced he thought he was. He knew all the details of the conspiracy and of

Lincoln's death, and he said his identity was a secret that's never been told except to me. The truth as to Lincoln's assassination may have been proved beyond doubt by the time this is found. Or perhaps he was really Booth. However, you who find this, spend the gold. Crauleia is yours, with its perhaps historic secret.' "

Gale handed the paper to Mr. Dilmous, blinking as if dazzled, and then poured the gold coins out into her hand. "I never saw any gold money before," she said.

"Let's count it," Jason said. He laid the coins out carefully on the inner lid of the box. Shelley, watching and silently reading the dates and words on the coins, felt the little ache again. Daddy was helping Jason count up their value. Daddy and Jason—not Shelley—though she was the one who recognized the crow's claw in the tree roots.

"Lots of these smaller ones are $5 and $10 gold pieces," Daddy said. "And this is a double eagle. It's $20. The face value of all the coins added together seems to be about $350. But of course they are far more valuable than that now, I should think."

"If he had really been Booth," Mr. Dilmous said, "the coins would have historic value that would make them practically priceless. But there was no story that Booth was paid anything for killing Lincoln. He was doing it for patriotic reasons, he thought.

"But this old man couldn't have really been Booth. There have been legends ever since the assassination that Booth escaped and was living somewhere in the South. Two or three different men besides this one, who claimed being Booth as they were dying, have already been checked out and the claims disproved. One I remember reading about was called Jack St. Helen, and another went by the name of Professor McFinnister.

"It was proved, though, that Booth was captured and killed while trying to escape from a barn where he was hiding— I think it was a man named Garret's tobacco barn."

"Mr. Dilmous must have total recall, from all the books he ever read," Jason whispered to Shelley.

"Not quite total," she whispered back. "He didn't recognize J. W. B. from the note, at first."

"I remember reading that Secretary of War Stanton sent ten different men," Mr. Dilmous went on, "to make sure the man who had been killed at the barn was Booth. The most positive identification was by a doctor who I think was named Dr. May. He had once cut a fibroid tumor from Booth's neck, and he knew the scar on the body was the one his operation left. I believe Booth's dentist also identified his teeth. His mother and his brother, and several of his friends, had no doubts it was John Wilkes Booth."

"Then why did anybody believe it wasn't?" Pam asked.

"If they wanted him to escape—" Shelley said, "maybe his mother and his brother had a reason to want people to think he was dead—"

"But the other witnesses didn't have that reason— at least, nobody thought they did at the time," Mr. Dilmous said. "Legends grow, that's all. Booth was killed; it was certain. But probably the government buried his body in secret and said very little about it, because they didn't want him to appear to be a martyr in the eyes of the South. Remember at that time there was still a lot of feeling about the War between the States. When Booth leaped onto the stage at Ford's Theater after he shot Lincoln—who was a good man, most Southerners know—he shouted the thing about tyrants, and 'The South is avenged!' So it would have been wise of Stanton not to give out much information about his burial. The secrecy, I suppose, led to the rumors that it wasn't Booth's body that was buried."

"But this poor old man *thought* he had killed Lincoln," Shelley said. "He really thought this money was what somebody in the conspiracy paid him for doing it. Where do you guess he got so many gold coins?"

"He might have collected them. Or he might have been paid for killing somebody else—and in his subconscious mind transferred the idea to Lincoln and Booth because he felt guilty. If he could feel patriotic instead, it might lighten his burden of guilt. But that's just guesswork. It would take a psychiatrist to build up that theory," Mr. Dilmous said.

"Well, at least I can see one reason why the note he wrote might have been hidden in the bedpost," Jason said. "Probably Mrs. Crawley found it after he died, and didn't want anybody to know his secret, but she thought she might sometime have to prove the money was rightfully hers. So it would be natural for her to hide the note that said he left it to her, but not destroy it."

"She did like to hide things," Bug said.

Gale said, "I have to go and tell my father! And show him the box and all. But I'll come right back." She clucked for Dracula. "I'm sure he'll be ready for you to buy Crauleia now, Mr. Calhoun," she told Daddy.

"We'll name it Crauleia Academy," Daddy said. "And we'll have to give you—and Michael and Patricia —scholarships to the school, for being such a help in acquiring it. You three can be our first students, along with my three."

"And Pam can come back every summer for summer school," Shelley said, thinking that Pam might be feeling left out.

"They may be our only students," Mama said dryly, "if you don't get the school finished and do some advertising."

"Back to work!" Daddy said. "Now that the great treasure hunt is over. Jason, want to help me cut up this old cedar?"

Gale waved and ran off toward home, Dracula zigzagging on his black wings above her. Pam and Bug went to fix Otto's and Grandma's lunch, while Mama fixed the family's. Mr. Dilmous said goodbye; he had to feed the gulls.

Shelley stood aside while Jason worked with Daddy, wishing Daddy had asked her to help too. She tried to tell herself it was because she wasn't any good with tools, but that didn't make her feel any better. Presently she wandered disconsolately down the woods path, to the Crow's Roost. She rationalized that her feeling was the normal letdown after such high excitement, and she knew she ought to be happy for Gale— and for Daddy. But she couldn't help feeling miserable. There was no getting around it; Jason had done the hard thing that made it possible to find the secret of the seven crows, not Shelley. It was Jason who had found the key and worked out the cipher that told where the box was. Shelley had only noticed the roots that looked like the crow's claw. It didn't take any brains to do that, she mourned, putting herself down though Jason himself had praised her. As Bug had said, it was Dracula who showed them the root, actually. A mere bird could do that.

But it was Jason, Shelley admitted fairly, who had made it possible for Daddy to buy Crauleia for the school. She told herself again that she wasn't jealous of Jason. She loved Jason, and she was proud to have a brother so clever and intelligent and resourceful and all the other good adjectives. But though she kept saying all this silently, when Shelley sat down on a log under the big tree she found herself crying. Hot tears ran down her face; she stifled sobs so that nobody would hear her crying. A hurting in the back of her throat made her feel like yowling. Something heavy pressed against her heart, inside.

Then she heard running footsteps. Instantly she stopped crying, hastily wiping her face against her shoulder because of course she hadn't a handkerchief or a tissue. It flashed through her mind that one disadvantage to wearing pants was that you had no underskirts to wipe your running nose on when you cried.

It was Gale, going back along the path to Crauleia. She couldn't miss seeing Shelley; she couldn't help seeing that Shelley had been crying.

Gale stopped abruptly at the Crows' Roost. "What's the matter?" she asked, while Dracula scolded and flew up to a tree branch. "Shelley, what's wrong?"

"Nothing. Nothing's wrong." But a word of sympathy sometimes made you start crying again. Shelley couldn't stop.

"Aren't you happy we found the secret? Aren't you glad my father's going to sell Crauleia to your Dad? He told me to tell Mr. Calhoun he could buy it any time now."

"Yes," Shelley gulped. "Of course I'm glad. But—" She sobbed, and couldn't stop herself from telling, "Oh, Gale, I know it's selfish and mean, but I wanted to be the one to get Crauleia for Daddy! Jason figured out the code. He loves Jason best—he lets Jason help him—he even lets Bug help more than he lets me. I've always wanted to do something so he'd love me as much as he does Jason—and I thought this was my big chance—and now I never can."

"Well!" Gale sat down on a log opposite Shelley, with her hands clasping her knees, and looked at

Shelley, scowling. "I thought you'd gotten over that silly idea. Jason and your dad both told you how great you were for having brilliant ideas about finding the secret. The code wasn't everything. Besides, I've figured out something since we talked about this before. I figure your dad sometimes favors Jason—and Bug —because he doesn't want them to catch on that he actually loves you best. You're his only girl, and fathers always love their girls a special way. He's trying to be fair. Fathers have to *seem* to love all their kids just the same, of course. So he has to bend over backwards to keep Jason and Bug from realizing how he really feels about you. I know; I've seen him look at you. It's the same way my father looks at me sometimes, and the way Roscoe looks at Patricia."

"You have? It is?" Astonished, Shelley stopped crying and thought about it. It might be—it might really be true, what Gale was saying! Looking back, she could see it might be. Gale was a realist; she wouldn't notice that special look, would she, unless it was true? She wouldn't be sentimental?

But Daddy had a special look for Jason, too, and a special way of rumpling Bug's hair. The way a father looks at his oldest son—and the way a father looks at his youngest child. . . She caught an elusive glimmer of perception and pinned it down in her mind; it was a new truth that she needed to know. It had been there all the time, too, if only she'd noticed.

"No," she found herself saying to Gale, then. "Thanks, Gale. You've made me understand something. But it's not exactly that he loves me best. I guess I don't really want him to—it wouldn't be right. It's just that he can love us all just as much—but not the same. A father's only human. He has to love each of us differently, that's all."

Suddenly she felt light and happy inside—she could soar like Dracula if only she had wings. "I'm such a stupid idiot," she said, standing up from the log. "And I bet I've got a million redbugs from sitting here in the middle of this Spanish moss. Come on, let's go tell Daddy what your father said about his buying Crauleia." She glanced shyly, then, into Gale's green eyes, and looked away. "Don't tell them I was crying, O.K.?"

"O.K.," Gale said.

They ran back to Crauleia together, Dracula zig-zagging overhead.

That night Jason and Shelley were doing the dishes after the others had gone upstairs. She had volunteered to take Bug's place; usually it was Jason's and Bug's job one night, Shelley's and Pam's the next. Tonight Shelley wanted to help Jason. It was good to feel happy again about him. It was good to know for sure that she needn't ever be jealous again, now that she could acknowledge to herself that maybe she had been.

"You know, Shell," Jason said, "I kind of wish we hadn't found it yet. Everything seems like an anti-climax now—nothing left to wonder about."

Bug and Pam came down to the kitchen then, to see what was keeping the other two so long.

"I've just got to train me a crow like Dracula," Bug said. "He was the one who really showed us where to dig for the treasure."

"I'll help you," Pam promised, "as soon as I train my pup. I'm going to name him Treasure."

Jason went on, "I kind of wish 'the secret that's never been told' were true—that Mr. Marcus hadn't been just a mental case. I guess I wish there was still something mysterious to wonder about, at Crauleia."

"So—how's this?" Shelley offered. She lowered her eyelids just a little, the way she had practiced in the mirror, until her eyes had hazel depths like secret pools in dark woods. She made her voice soft and breathless with possibility. "Did you look at the dates on the coins? I did. They were all minted *before* 1865."

"You mean—" Jason said, his eyes beginning to shine, "if he wasn't Booth and collected the coins later, when he was getting old and losing his mind, in order to pretend to himself that he was paid them for killing Lincoln—"

"Yes," Shelley said, "it stands to reason some of them would have had later dates if he wasn't Booth. But if he was Booth and had been paid in 1865 with those particular coins, not one of them *could* have been dated any later."

"Of course it could be just chance," Jason said. "But —all those people who identified the body as Booth's

could have been lying, for some reason of their own—
maybe to help him get away. We'll never know. And
if he *was* Booth," he went on thoughtfully, "he didn't
really get away, even if he lived to be old. He was
punished anyway. Maybe that's why he got to be a
mental case, tormented by feeling guilty for killing a
good man like Lincoln. You have to know he felt
awful about it, the way he wrote about never being
able to spend the 'blood money.' "

"Maybe it really is a secret that's never been told,"
Shelley said, "except to us and Mrs. Howard Townsend
Crawley."

"Maybe," Jason said.

He looked as if he believed it. Well, that's why
such legends live on, Shelley thought. Because people
like to believe they know mysterious secrets.

About the Author

WYLLY FOLK ST. JOHN's books are all set in the South, where she has always lived. *The Mystery of the Other Girl* takes place on the Florida Gulf Coast and *The Secret of the Seven Crows* on the Gulf Coast of Mississippi. All her other books are set in Georgia. She always writes about real children, giving them exciting fictional adventures.

Mrs. St. John was born in South Carolina, spent her childhood in Savannah, and was graduated from the University of Georgia in Athens. She now lives in Social Circle, Georgia—a small town not far from Atlanta. Mrs. St. John has for many years been a staff writer for *The Atlanta Journal and Constitution Magazine*. A number of her short stories and articles, as well as five adult novels, have been published in national magazines. She was named Georgia Author of the Year in 1968, and in 1973 her book, *Uncle Robert's Secret,* was named a runner-up for the Edgar Allan Poe Award by the Mystery Writers of America.